KT-212-606

HOW TO AVOID CERTAIN DEATH

BY SEBILLIUS QUARK

(Discovered wrapped in a really,
really old pair of underpants, in a
really, really old chest, in the attic
of a really, really old house by
TOM CLEMPSON.)

SCHOLASTIC

Scholastic Children's Books
An imprint of Scholastic Ltd
Euston House, 24 Eversholt Street, London, NW1 1DB, UK
Registered office: Westfield Road, Southam, Warwickshire, CV47 0RA
SCHOLASTIC and associated logos are trademarks and/
or registered trademarks of Scholastic Inc.

First published in the UK by Scholastic Ltd, 2017

Text copyright © Tom Clempson, 2017
Illustration copyright © Jason Cockcroft, 2017

The rights of Tom Clempson and Jason Cockcroft to be identified as
the author and illustrator of this work have been asserted by them.

ISBN 978 1407 17225 5

A CIP catalogue record for this book
is available from the British Library.

All rights reserved.
This book is sold subject to the condition that it shall not, by
way of trade or otherwise, be lent, hired out or otherwise circulated in
any form of binding or cover other than that in which it is published. No
part of this publication may be reproduced, stored in a retrieval system,
or transmitted in any form or by any means (electronic, mechanical,
photocopying, recording or otherwise) without prior
written permission of Scholastic Limited.

Printed by CPI Group (UK) Ltd, Croydon, CR0 4YY
Papers used by Scholastic Children's Books are made
from wood grown in sustainable forests.

1 3 5 7 9 10 8 6 4 2

This is a work of fiction. Names, characters, places, incidents
and dialogues are products of the author's imagination or are used
fictitiously. Any resemblance to actual people, living or dead,
events or locales is entirely coincidental.

www.scholastic.co.uk

For my entire great big family. All the way from King Bubbubs to Princesses Iris and Martha of Nappy Land.

Goldland

The Firs
Sea

some Islands

Scott's
Lan

The Angerland Sea

Kinder

Angerland

Island

The Seventh
Sea

Bubbubs

Under water
Island

Witch Island

The Small Sea

Land With no name

Watermala

South Land With no name

The Water Channel

The Fifth Sea

Hedgehog Island

Ozz

The Small Defenceless Island

The South Sea

terly

The United Lands of Division

N
W E
S

THE BEGINNING

Once upon a time, there was a beautiful kingdom called Angerland, where water nymphs frolicked, where unicorns pranced, and where a very special princess fell in love with a...

ERGHH! YUCK! No! Forget it. I forgot how terrible the beginning of this story is. It needs a *great* beginning. After all, this is the sixth greatest story never to have been told! Let's start at the best part of all – *the end...*

THE END

And then he died.

The End

Wait!

What am I doing? That's almost as bad as the beginning!

OK, let's do this again, and this time I promise it'll be good.

I'm going to start this story at the perfect place — two and a half pages *before* the beginning.

TWO AND A
HALF PAGES BEFORE
THE BEGINNING

THE REAL,
GENUINE, OFFICIAL,
PROPER BEGINNING

Sarah and Charlie were both ten years old. They were twins. And they grew up in a time and place where fairy tales were true; where pirates ruled the seas, kings and queens ruled the lands, and magicians ruled lines in books, using their rulers. That's right – it was a time when magic was real, romance was even more real, and danger was really, really real, with really real cherries on top (none of those weird, sugary glacé cherry things).

But Sarah and Charlie didn't get to experience any of this. That's because they lived in the most boring and empty cottage, in the most boring and empty forest, in the most boring and empty corner of Angerland. There were no towns or villages nearby, and the nearest neighbour lived over two hundred elephants away ("elephants" was how they measured things in Angerland, just like they measure things in feet, hands and centipedes in other parts of the world).

In fact, Sarah and Charlie had never met a single other human being apart from their grandma Ethel and grandpa Harold, who they lived with in their little cottage. Sounds *super* boring, right? Well, it kind of *wasn't*, because most of their days were filled with stuff like *this*...

"Run!" barked Grandpa Harold as Sarah and Charlie raced through the woods, closely followed by Grandpa Harold and Grandma Ethel and a bright green parrot. "The wolves are coming!"

"They're almost here!" shrieked Grandma Ethel. "They're right behind us!"

A loud howling filled the woods.

The twins ran as fast as they could, desperately searching for a tree they could climb, or a fallen branch to use as a weapon, but they were moving so quickly everything was just a blur. They were panting hard, gasping for breath. They knew the wolves must be close behind, but neither of them dared to look back. And then they heard it, a noise from behind that filled them with panic – a loud *THUD* followed by a cry of pain.

Sarah braved a glance over her shoulder and, to her horror, saw that Grandma Ethel had tripped and fallen. Sarah skidded to a halt. She raced to Ethel's aid, helped her to her feet, and then –

The wolves caught up with her.

A huge, salivating beast was on top of her in a heartbeat, its teeth bared, rage in its eyes. Sarah was knocked off her feet, sent flying through the air, then landed on her back with a painful *CRUNCH*.

Every bird in the forest, apart from a vibrant green parrot who had been watching on in horror, took to the skies as the beast lunged in for the kill.

Sarah's scream pierced the air.

"Grandpa!" Sarah squealed. "That tickles! Stop! No more!"

"Grrrrrrrr!" said Grandpa Harold, who was on all fours, doing his best impression of a wolf, shaking Sarah's arm with her sleeve between his teeth and growling loudly.

There were no real wolves at all. No real danger. No real chase. That's because this was a Thursday. Thursdays were always the days when Harold and Ethel would give Sarah and Charlie lessons in "Running Away" – this usually consisted of Harold pretending to be a band of ruthless pirates, or a horde of flesh-eating zombies, or a pack of ravenous animals (like today), and Sarah and Charlie would have to run away from him. It was all part of their ongoing survival training. Survival training was a big part of Sarah and Charlie's lives. Most other children's lives were made up of:

1. Going to school.
2. Playing games.
3. Lazing around.

But Sarah and Charlie's lives were a bit different. *Their* lives were made up of:

1. Survival training.

2. A bit more survival training.

3. Even more survival training.

Their grandparents taught them a different survival activity for every day of the week: Mondays were for sword-fighting lessons, Tuesdays were for hunting practice, Wednesdays were for building the Boat of Destiny (which all four of them had been building together as a family ever since the twins were babies), Fridays were for den-building lessons, Saturdays were for learning how to lay traps and hide, and Sundays were spent learning the history of their country – Angerland. So as you can see, Sarah and Charlie were hardly ever bored. (Except maybe on a Sunday when Grandma Ethel droned on and on about the royal family of Angerland, and the *history* of the royal family of Angerland, and the *duties* of the royal family of Angerland, and the *names of the pets* of the royal family of Angerland…)

Thursdays, on the other hand, were *never* boring.

"If your grandpa had been a *real* wolf, you'd be

dead!" shouted Grandma Ethel as she marched towards Sarah, who was still flat on her back, whilst Harold continued to pretend to chew her arm off. "You broke the First Rule of Running Away – you have to RUN AWAY! Never. Turn. Back! I tell you time and time again, but you just don't seem to listen."

"Ha ha! You lose! I win!" cheered Charlie, doing a little bum-wiggling victory dance in front of Sarah.

"Oh really?" sneered Sarah, still flat on her back. "Well, who won last week, when your legs got too tired to keep running from the killer goats and I had to give you a piggyback? Or in den-building, when you needed a little nap, and I had to finish building your entire den for you? Or in sword fighting, when you had to stop for a snack break and ate my entire packed lunch? Did you win then? No. The only thing you're winning at is being the most spoilt little baby in the whole world, because Grandma lets you get away with *anything*, all because you used to be the smallest! Well, now you're the *tallest*, and I still have to do everything for you!"

Charlie wasn't wiggling his bum and celebrating any more. He was staring at the ground, his face red with shame and anger. Sarah was right, and he knew it. Sarah didn't feel good about this – in fact she felt kind of guilty – but these things needed to be said, and she couldn't hold them in any longer.

"It's all pointless!" Sarah shouted at her grandma. "It's pointless Charlie spending every single day of his life learning to survive life-threatening situations when all he's really learning is how to come running to me for help! And it's pointless *either of us* spending every single day of our lives learning to survive life-threatening situations, when none of these life-threatening situations ever actually happen! EVER! It feels like we're training for something that isn't even real – an adventure that never arrives! We've got all these skills, but we never get a chance to use them! It's like … it's like… It's like having the world's best sledge, but never having any snow to use it on, or… No! It's like spending your whole life building a boat when your grandparents tell you every single day that you should never go near the water! It's all a massive waste of time and it's *pointless*! All of it!"

Ethel stood over Sarah, and calmly crossed her arms.

"Are you done?" she asked softly. "Or is there anything else you'd like to add?"

"Actually, there *is* something else," Sarah growled tempestuously.

"And what would that be?" asked Ethel.

"Can you please tell Grandpa to stop chewing my arm?"

"Oop! Sorry!" Harold chuckled as he spat Sarah's sleeve from his mouth and got up from his hands and knees. "Got a bit carried away! Deep in character. Lost in the moment. Grrrr! Woof! Ha ha!" Harold then noticed the stern look on Ethel's face, and instantly stopped chuckling. "Sorry, darling. Carry on."

"Sarah," Ethel said slowly, with wide, serious

eyes, "I will tell you the same thing I always tell you — you are preparing for *the unknown*."

"But *what* unknown?" Sarah demanded.

"We don't know, darling," Ethel explained softly. "That's why it's unknown. "All we know is that you and Charlie will one day play an extremely important role in this world, more important than you can ever imagine, and, when that day comes, everything you've learned will come of use, the Boat of Destiny will come of use, and you will thank us for these survival lessons."

"How do you know all of this if it's so unknown?" Sarah asked, her forehead crinkled in confusion.

"We just know," said Ethel, breaking eye contact with Sarah, the way she always did when she did that annoying "grown-ups" thing of not giving a proper answer to a perfectly simple question.

"*How?*" asked Sarah. "That doesn't make any sense! There's something you're not telling us, and I know it! Why won't you just tell us the truth?!"

Ethel replied with another classic, full-on,

annoying grown-up shutdown:

"I think that's enough questions for one day."

"No!" Sarah argued. "I want to know what—"

"Turn your collar up, dear, I can see your birthmark," Ethel interrupted. "You *know* how disastrous it would be if anyone ever saw your birthmark!"

Every member of the family had the same seal-shaped birthmark on the back of their necks, and, for some reason (a reason that only Harold and Ethel knew), keeping this covered up at all times was just as important as learning to run away, build dens, fight with swords, and all that other stuff.

"Now, how about you two go and finish painting the final decorations on the outside of the Boat of Destiny while your grandpa and I go back to the cottage and get lunch started?" suggested Grandma Ethel as Sarah angrily pulled her collar up.

"Are you serious?" Charlie squealed with excitement.

"Yes, but don't be long. Food will be ready in half an hour. If you're speedy, we might even have time for a quick board game before this afternoon's training."

Charlie raced off through the bluebell-filled woods, his lanky legs leaping over the flowers on his way to the Boat of Destiny, whilst Sarah grudgingly trudged on behind, doing her best to hide her excitement at actually getting to finish painting the signs they had been designing every evening, in their beds, for the past nine weeks. It was hard to believe that, after ten whole years, today was actually going to be the day that the Boat of Destiny would finally be finished. They weren't usually allowed to work on the boat on any day other than Wednesdays, so to be allowed to do this on a *Thursday* felt like an extra-special treat.

Sarah and Charlie hadn't been this excited since they had both received bows and arrows for their tenth birthdays. However, their spirits may not have been quite so high had they known what was lurking around the corner – just a stone's throw away, stalking through the woods, *the unknown* was heading straight towards the cottage, waiting to obliterate their peaceful lives.

THE UNKNOWN

All their lives, Sarah and Charlie had been taught
to live by three unbreakable rules:

1. Stay away from strangers.
2. Always keep your birthmarks covered up.

And here's the weird bit...

3. Never go anywhere near the sea. EVER!

"Stay. Away. From the sea!" Harold and Ethel would remind them almost every single day. "The sea is full of pirates and sharks and, worse than both of those things – *SHARK PIRATES!!!*" (Shark pirates didn't actually exist; Harold and Ethel just made them up because they *reaaalllly* wanted to make sure Sarah and Charlie stayed away from the sea.)

"If we're not allowed near the sea, I still don't really get why we've built a boat," Charlie said to Sarah as he finished painting the words "The Ship of Destiny", in huuuuge bubble-writing across the back of the beautiful, polished, golden-brown boat.

"It's all because of Mum and Dad," Sarah told Charlie as she stood back to admire the gigantic sea serpent she had painted down one side of the ship. "Grandma and Grandpa want to sail off to find that island..."

"The Island of Lovely, Cuddly..."

"The Island of Unbelievably Cute and Fluffy Bunnies," Sarah corrected him. "You really should know it by now, Charlie. Grandpa's stitched it inside every pair of shoes you've ever owned!"

"Oh yeah, right," said Charlie, slipping one of his shoes off to see the message that was stitched into the insole:

IN CASE OF EMERGENCY:

- *Go to the Island of Unbelievably Cute and Fluffy Bunnies.*
- *Find the magical meadow at the centre of the island.*
- *You may make ONE wish, which will instantly come true.*

"And blah, blah, blah. It's all a load of rubbish," said Sarah as she playfully flicked a dollop of paint on Charlie's shoe. "If that place actually existed, someone would have found it by now and would be selling maps to it, for one hundred gold coins each. I think Grandma and Grandpa want to believe it's true, so that they can wish that nothing ever happened to Mum and Dad, and we could have them back."

Sarah and Charlie couldn't remember their parents, and whenever they asked Harold and Ethel about them, they always got the same "That's enough questions for one day" answer. The only thing Sarah and Charlie did know about their mum and dad was that something very bad had happened to them not long after Sarah and Charlie had been born, something involving pirates, and this was why Harold and Ethel had raised them.

Birds sang gently in the trees, warm spring sunshine dappled the forest floor, and the paintbrushes rattled noisily in the wooden bucket as Sarah and Charlie made their way back towards the cottage from the secret hillside where the boat was hidden. Had the paintbrushes rattled just a teeeensy bit quieter, Sarah and Charlie would have heard the dozens of footsteps that were marching through the woods, not too far away. They would have heard the distant scuffle that had taken place outside the cottage, and the faint, muffled cries of two people who were being tied up.

"We finished it!" Sarah cheered as she and Charlie burst noisily into the quaint little ivy-covered stone cottage, followed by the bright green parrot who swooped in through an open window.

They were met by the delicious smell of stew and dumplings, but Harold and Ethel were nowhere to be seen. Sarah knew exactly where they would be, though – out in the vegetable garden, picking herbs to add to the pot.

"The boat's all done! When can we take it out on the water?" Sarah called out through the open back door whilst Charlie lifted the lid off the cook pot and took a long sniff of the glorious-smelling steam that billowed out from it.

"Sarah!" Charlie called in terrified silence.

"Are you two deaf?" Sarah yelled, not hearing Charlie's whisper. "I said we finished it! It's done! Ten long years of hard work is finally over! Can we do something special to celebrate? Is the

Fammelberry Fizz ready to drink yet?"

But no one replied except for Charlie, who had finally found his voice.

"SARAAAAAH!" he bellowed.

Sarah came rushing back into the kitchen to see the stew boiling over on the stove, and Charlie standing next to it with a piece of paper in his hand.

"What are you *doing*?!" Sarah gasped as she raced to remove the stew from the heat. "Did you not see it boiling over?"

"Look!" Charlie said, thrusting the piece of paper in front of Sarah's face.

As Sarah read the note, she didn't notice how hot the handle of the pot was in her hands. She didn't notice it slipping from her grasp. And she didn't even notice the whole thing crashing to the cobblestone floor and spilling out around their feet.

She didn't notice any of this because the writing on the note had just taken her life as she knew it, tipped it upside down, and emptied the contents of it on to the floor, along with the ruined stew.

DEAR CHILDREN,

ON THE ORDERS OF MY CAPTAIN, VLADIMIR
DEATH PIRATE EVIL LORD OF THE SEVEN SEAS,
WE HAVE TAKEN YOUR GRANDPARENTS ON
OUR PIRATE SHIP, THE VLADIATOR, AND HAVE
LOCKED THEM IN OUR DUNGEON THING,
WHERE THEY WILL SUFFER FOR THE REST OF
THEIR LIVES (DON'T WORRY, THOUGH, THEY
PROBABLY WON'T SUFFER FOR LONG — MOST
OF OUR PRISONERS ONLY LAST A FEW DAYS
AS WE USUALLY FORGET TO FEED THEM). WE
APOLOGIZE FOR ANY INCONVENIENCE THIS
MAY CAUSE.

YOURS SINCERELY,
FIRST MATE NED

The fear that crept through Charlie's body started in his stomach, then radiated outwards like quick-spreading frost, causing him to shake all over. His cold, numb fingertips trembled so much that the note fell from his hand and joined the rest of the mess on the kitchen floor.

"Is this ... *it*?" he managed to whisper. "Is this the *unknown*?"

But for once in her life Sarah didn't have an answer for Charlie.

"What do we do?"

Again Sarah had no answer. All of their training had taught them that when the unknown arrived, they had to run, hide and defend themselves if necessary. But now that the moment was here, all that training felt wrong. It didn't feel like they should run *away* from the pirates and let them get away with their grandparents. It felt like they ought to run *after* them, and *help* their grandparents — exactly what Harold and Ethel had told them they should never do.

"Sarah? What do we do?" Charlie repeated, growing worried by the length of time it was taking Sarah to reply.

"We go after them, of course," she said quite bluntly. "We find this Vladimir Death Pirate, and we get Grandma and Grandpa back."

"We ... we go *after* them? Are you crazy? They're PIRATES!" wailed Charlie. "There's NO WAY the two of us can defeat an entire boatful of pirates!"

"You're probably right," Sarah said calmly, "but we have to try. Get your things together and let's go."

"Get my things together? We're heading straight towards certain death! What am I supposed to pack, a *coffin*?"

"Don't worry," said Sarah confidently, "I've got a plan."

A CHAPTER ABOUT NOTHING

So there we have it, the beginning has officially begun. Or has it just ended? I don't know, I'm new to this whole storytelling thing. All I do know is that you shouldn't waste your time reading a chapter about nothing. You should be moving rapidly along to find out more about this pirate who was responsible for Harold and Ethel's kidnapping...

THE PIRATE WHO WAS RESPONSIBLE FOR HAROLD AND ETHEL'S KIDNAPPING

Vladimir was his name, and piracy was his game. (Well, actually, it wasn't a *game*, it was more of a *business*, but that doesn't rhyme as nicely.) He was an *evil* pirate, a lord of death, who sailed the seven seas. And that's why they called him Vladimir Death Pirate: Evil Lord of the Seven Seas. (Which is a little bit too descriptive if you ask me, but that's just my opinion.)

He was a pirate so terrible and mean that people sang scary songs about him, children had nightmares about him, and one particularly clever and talented individual even wrote a rather amazing book about him (you should read it sometime, page 25 is particularly good!). This pirate created chaos and wreaked havoc wherever he went, and was responsible for some of the greatest atrocities in history, including the Terrible Eye-Poking of the Pygmy Meerkats of Watermala, the Horrific International Owl-Mocking Disaster, and the now infamous events that took place on the Island of Unbelievably Cute and Fluffy Bunnies (but more about that later).

Vladimir Death Pirate (I can't be bothered calling him Vladimir Death Pirate: Evil Lord of the Seven Seas over and over again) stood at the very front of his big, black ship, the *Vladiator*, with his long black cloak billowing in the wind, and a tatty old map of the world clutched under one arm as he surveyed his crew, who were busily scrubbing the decks for the fourth hour in a row whilst Vladimir (I can't be bothered calling him Vladimir Death

Pirate over and over again) barked orders at them, like: "Keep scrubbing, you filthy swines!" and "You must be the laziest crew of all time!" and "We're sailing away from a sponge!" (don't worry yourself about that last one – not all of his orders made a whole lot of sense).

Then, just after Vlad (I can't be bothered calling him Vladimir over and over again) had ordered Gigantic Steve (the largest living pirate) to throw Hard-Working Pamela (the hardest-working living pirate) overboard for being too lazy, the *Vladiator* suddenly lurched to a crunching halt as it smashed into a huge rock that had been hiding amongst the waves. With a large hole now in the side of the ship, Vlad and his crew took the rowing boats to a nearby forest, where they went in search of some timber to repair the damage.

The crew had been searching the bluebell-filled forest for hours, and had found many pieces of wood that seemed perfect for the job, but every time they showed these finds to Vlad he bellowed things like "NO GOOD!" or "RUBBISH! YOU'RE ALL IDIOTS! KEEP LOOKING!" so the crew continued to search, and Vlad continued to get angrier and angrier, until they came across a small cottage in the woods, where an old man and woman were making what smelled like the world's best stew.

"That silly little parrot's here again!" Harold called to Ethel, whilst he laid the dinner table. "And I think it's... AAAARGHHH!"

Harold stumbled back in shock, dropping the dinner plates to the floor and shrieking in terror at what he saw outside the window – there, out in the woods, where they hadn't seen a single other soul in over ten years, were dozens and dozens of nasty-looking pirates, all peering in through the windows.

"ETHEL!" Harold screamed. "PIRATES!"

As quick as a flash, Ethel had her sword in her hand, and was shuttering all the windows, locking the front door, and peering out through a tiny little spyhole.

"*Are* you pirates?" she called to the burly gang outside.

"No, no!" replied Vlad.

(This wasn't exactly true.)

"Who are you then?" she demanded.

"We're Good Samaritans, giving gold to the poor," said Vlad.

(This was also not exactly true.)

"Oh. Really? Well, what brings you to our

woods?" Ethel asked, not sounding quite so hostile any more.

"We came to hide wood so we could destroy our boat," Vlad explained.

(Not only was this not true, but it didn't even make the slightest bit of sense!)

"We're just looking for some materials, me lady," First Mate Ned quickly clarified. "To repair a hole in our ship. We don't mean you no harm."

"Well, we have plenty of wood left over from building our own boat," Harold kindly informed them as he unlocked the door and stepped out to greet them. "It's just round the back, in the garden shed. We've even got some nails if you need them!"

The pirates gratefully helped themselves to the stacks of ready-cut timber, then thanked Harold and Ethel with hugs and handshakes before trudging back towards their rowing boats.

"Well, that was a stroke of luck!" First Mate Ned laughed as he and Vlad followed on behind the crew. "Two of the most generous people I've ever come across! I feel like we ought to repay them in some way, as a thank you, don't you reckon?"

Vlad paused and thought about this for a moment.

Then he thought a bit more.

And a little bit more.

And then he came up with the perfect idea:

"I HATE them! Let's lock 'em in our dungeon thing for the rest of their lives!"

This wasn't exactly the kind of thank you that Ned had had in mind, but an order was an order, so, whilst Vlad and the crew returned to the *Vladiator* to repair the hole, Ned went back to the cottage, tied Harold and Ethel in ropes, then locked them in the *Vladiator*'s dungeon thing, where, yet again, Vlad was about to do something *very* unexpected.

THE TRUTH ABOUT VLAD

It won't surprise you to hear that Vlad was a baddie. There was no denying it. I mean, they don't call him Vladimir Death Pirate: Evil Lord of the Seven Seas for nothing, you know! (I can't believe I had to write his *whole* name out *again*). You just heard about how he had his hardest-working crew member thrown overboard for not working hard enough. He had Harold and Ethel kidnapped and locked up in a cage in the hold of the ship for doing nothing but being kind. And let's not even mention the atrocities that occurred on the Island of Unbelievably Cute and Fluffy Bunnies (I promise I'll explain all that later).

But if you're very clever (and I'm sure you are ... maybe) you might have noticed that something about Vlad seems ... well, *wrong*.

I said at the end of the last chapter that he was about to do something very unexpected, but in actual fact, Vlad did unexpected things so often that his crew expected the unexpected at the most unexpected times. They always expected him to do something that didn't make sense, give an order that seemed like the meanest, worst idea ever, or say something that was just altogether brain-meltingly stupid.

Well, there was a very good reason why Vlad did all of these strange things, and that reason began way, way back, when Vlad was a freshly stolen baby...

WAY, WAY, BACK WHEN VLAD WAS A FRESHLY STOLEN BABY

Many years ago there was a pirate known simply as Death.

Now, it's important to understand that not all pirates are evil. There's a sliding scale. Some pirates are good, some of them are not so good, and others are downright horrible.

Well, Death was nothing like any of these pirates. He was simply the worst pirate who ever lived. When I say he was the "worst" pirate, I don't mean he was no good as a pirate; I mean he was the wickedest, cruellest pirate there was.

He had metal nails for teeth, hideous claws for hands, and eyes that blazed like the fires of damnation (in a bluey/greenish kind of way). And Death had only one desire – **WORLD DOMINATION!** He had spent all his life trying to become the world's most rich and powerful man, but no matter how many people he killed, or how much gold he stole, **WORLD DOMINATION** always seemed to be just out of his grasp. He'd tried *everything* – he'd hired the most dangerous crew, destroyed countless cities, and even had a freshly picked bouquet of four-leaf clovers delivered to his cabin, every day, for good luck – but **WORLD DOMINATION** continued to elude him. So, one day, Death decided it was time to take his efforts to the next level, and did the most drastic thing imaginable – he visited a *fortune teller*!

Now, there were two fortune tellers in the area, both of whom happened to be witches. The first of these fortune-telling witches was named the Wicked Witch of Just East of the North-West, who was famous for having every single one of her fortune-telling prophecies come true (and also famous for not being very good at spells). The other fortune-telling witch was named Grimelda the Pure of Heart, who was famous for being kind of OK at doing spells (but not so good with prophecies). So, since it was a prophecy that Death was after, he went to visit the Wicked Witch of Just East of the North-West in her grubby little manure-scented tent, on the muddy shores of the grey and dreary Witch Island.

"World domination?" laughed the Wicked Witch, who was so gruesome and covered in boils and pus that Death could hardly bear to look at her. "Easy! I'll write you out a prophecy. You'll need to follow the directions of this prophecy very carefully, and within two weeks your world domination problem should be all cleared up."

The Wicked Witch's prophecy said that, in order to achieve **WORLD DOMINATION**, Death needed to steal a child, a particular child, from a particular part of the world, and she even gave him a map, marked with an *X*, to show him exactly where to find this child. Just how, exactly, stealing a child was going to help him on his quest for **WORLD DOMINATION**, Death had no idea. The entire prophecy made no sense to him whatsoever, but then again, most things that witches did made no sense to him (like burying a bat in a bucket of worms to help you sleep better at night!). But Death knew that this witch's prophecies *always* came true, so he decided not to question it. He followed the Wicked Witch's prophecy to the letter, and seven days later he had stolen himself a little baby boy.

Two weeks passed, and Death still hadn't achieved **WORLD DOMINATION.** Two *months* passed – no **WORLD DOMINATION.** Two *years* passed, but **WORLD DOMINATION** was *still* nowhere to be found! Death went back to Witch Island, to try to get his money back, but the Wicked Witch and her grubby little tent were no longer there. So now, with a two-year-old boy to look after, Death decided there was only one way this child could possibly bring

WORLD DOMINATION – he would have to raise the boy as his son, and teach him to be the most evil pirate imaginable, and then he could *help* Death dominate the world the good old-fashioned way – with lots more death, destruction and downright naughtiness!

Death named his son "Vlad", and spent years training him in acts of cruelty, barbarism and general evilness. Even when Vlad was just a baby Death gave him a cannon and tried to teach him to shoot it at innocent penguins.

But as Vlad grew older and was able to talk and do things for himself, Death was in for some shocking and unsettling news – Vlad was *not like Death in the slightest*! In fact, he was the exact opposite. He was the most *un*-evil evil son Death could ever have hoped for, which was why Death's Ship, the *Death Ship*, was filled with exchanges like this...

"C'mon, boy," Death would growl. "Let's go eat live scorpions!"

"No thanks, Dad," Vlad would reply with a polite smile. "I'd rather stay here and paint some pictures of beautiful butterflies." (Little Vlad *loved* animals.)

"It's nearly seven forty-two," Death would cheer excitedly every evening. "Let's go boil some old ladies and make Old Lady Stew!"

"Maybe tomorrow, Dad," was Little Vlad's daily response. "I'm going to stay here and find some cute and furry animals to cuddle." (Vlad *really* loved animals.)

Death would have been a laughing stock if anyone else had heard his evil son talking in such an un-evil manner. So, when Vlad was five years old, Death decided to take Vlad's training to the next level, and did the most drastic thing imaginable – he took him to see a *fortune teller*! Well, a fortune teller who was good at spells, to be precise. The only fortune teller who was any good with spells was a witch named Grimelda the Pure of Heart (the one who was famous for being kind of OK at doing spells, but not so good at prophecies), so Death went and paid her a visit, in her little wooden shack, in the semi-gloomy hilltops of Witch Island, to see if she could *magic* some evil into the boy!

"Put a curse on a little boy? What kind of witch do you take me for?" sneered the not-so-gruesome-as-the-wicked-witch-but-still-quite-yucky witch, who Death could just about manage to look at without being sick. "I don't put curses on people! I only use my powers for good! I brew remedies, tell fortunes, make prophecies, give fashion tips, but I don't *curse* people! Now get out of my house before I turn you into a bogey!"

"You misunderstand me, witch," Death assured her with a simpering smile. "My son is ill, and I need you to fix him," he lied.

"Well, why didn't you say so? What's wrong with him?"

"He always says the exact opposite of what I want him to sa— I mean, he always says the exact opposite of what *he* wants to say," Death lied some more.

So, believing Death's lies, the witch Grimelda took pity on poor little Vlad, and cooked up a spell to make him say the exact opposite of what he meant to say.

Twenty minutes later, Death's wish had finally come true – Vlad was talking like a normal evil pirate, and the best part was – *he didn't even realize he was doing it.*

So when Vlad thought he was saying:

"Oh, aren't baby seals delightful! I wish I could

have one to cuddle and kiss for the rest of my life," he was actually saying: "Aren't baby seals disgusting! I wish I could smash them all with broken shopping trolleys, until they're nothing but seal soup!"

Whenever he met new people, instead of saying, "Hello, pleased to meet you", Vlad would always say: "Get out of my way, you ugly great burp!"

If he was feeling a little bit lonely, or sad, instead of saying, "Please can I have a cosy snuggle?" he would say, "Leave me alone, before I rip your stinking elbows off!"

If he wanted to say something funny, he accidentally said something sad. If he tried to be polite, he accidentally said something rude. And if he wanted to say something kind, he ended up saying something monstrously mean, without even noticing he was doing it. "Sad" meant "happy", "hate" meant "love", and "poke you with extremely sharp and pointy pieces of dried dog poo" meant "kiss".

It was the greatest plan Death had ever come up with.

Vlad had no idea that he was saying the opposite of what he meant, and he could never understand why everyone always did the opposite of what he asked, or why they always shouted at him when he said "hello", or why they screamed when he wanted to cuddle them, or why they ran away as fast as they could when he asked to kiss their babies. So Vlad steered clear of other people, and only felt comfortable around his dad and his toys, because they were the only ones who ever understood him.

At first, Death was over the moon at how horribly his son had learned to speak, but he soon realized that his extremely clever plan wasn't as clever as he had thought — you see, even though Vlad had stopped *saying* nice things, it hadn't stopped him from *doing* nice things:

• Vlad continued to make soft toys out of old rags instead of joining Death on his puppy-hunting expeditions, and Death's dreams of **WORLD DOMINATION** slipped one elephant further from his reach.

- Vlad continued to paint beautiful pictures of butterflies and fairies instead of burning orphanages to the ground, and Death's dreams of **WORLD DOMINATION** slipped *another* elephant out of reach.

- Vlad continued to knit dresses for all of the rats on board the *Death Ship* instead of sneaking lions into the kitchen cupboards of sleeping old ladies, and Death's dreams of **WORLD DOMINATION** drifted so far from his reach that he eventually came to the conclusion that he must have stolen the wrong baby, because Vlad was never going to make it as a proper pirate. He was never going to be evil. And he was certainly not going to help Death in his quest for **WORLD DOMINATION.** All these years of training had been a total waste of time. So, deciding to cut his losses, Death took the most reasonable course of action he could think of – he would abandon Vlad, in the middle of nowhere, in the middle of the night, whilst he was fast asleep. That night, whilst Vlad was snuggled in his bed, sound asleep and cuddled up to his favourite, home-made toy bunny, Death quietly lifted Vlad from his bed, placed him in a small rowing boat, and then pushed little Vlad out to sea with nothing but a two-day-old cheese sandwich, a thimbleful of water, and a dirty old rag for a blanket.

"So, what's the plan, now, Cap'n?" Death's first mate asked, the next morning.

"We start again, from scratch," Death growled miserably to his big, muscly brute of a first mate, who had a surprisingly pretty pink bow in her hair. "We go all the way back to where the map is marked with an *X*, we steal the *correct* child, and then we get on with this whole **WORLD DOMINATION** thing."

"Right you are, Cap'n," grunted Pink Bow Pirate. "When do we start?"

"Right now," said Death. "Pass me the map from my desk."

"Erm…" said Pink Bow Pirate, staring blankly at Death's desk. "I don't see no map, just this dirty old rag you was gonna give Vlad for a blanket."

Death jumped to his feet. He dashed to his desk. He snatched up the dirty old rag, searched everywhere for the map, and then he threw his desk across the room when he realized the mistake he had made...

Thousands of elephants away, the golden sun was just peeking over the horizon, and Vlad woke up to find that he was in a tiny little boat in the middle of the ocean, and he was all alone. He cried and he sobbed and he wailed.

"Yippee," he whimpered, heartbroken. "I'm so happy! Woohoo!"

But as he dried his eyes on his rag of a blanket, he realized that his rag of a blanket was not a rag of a blanket at all — it was a *map*. A map marked with a big, black *X*!

Vlad instantly stopped crying, and a smile slowly broke out across his face. He knew what was happening! (Except he didn't.) His dad had set him a challenge! (He hadn't.) It was just like in January, when Death had left him for two days, on a rock, in the middle of the ocean, with nothing but a kitten and a mallet, to see if Vlad might get hungry enough to smash the kitten, and eat it! (He didn't. And it wasn't.)

I know how to find my dad! Vlad thought excitedly. *He will be waiting for me where* X *marks the spot!* (He wouldn't.)

So Vlad and Death both began searching at the very same time. Vlad was searching for the love and understanding that only a family member can provide, and Death was searching for the **WORLD DOMINATION** *-ness* that only his map could provide. He spent so much time and energy searching for that map that he all but disappeared from the world of pirating. Many thought he must have retired, or that maybe he was even *dead*. But he was neither. He was just searching.

And thirty years later, he and Vlad were *still* searching.

Stoppety, stoppety, stop! Vlad had a map marked with a big *X*, yet he still hadn't found his dad after thirty years of searching? How difficult could it be! Well, *very* difficult actually. You see, first of all, you have to remember that the map *didn't* lead back to Death, it led to the place where Death had stolen Vlad as a baby. Secondly, even if the map was of any use to him, Vlad could never make sense of it because his tears had managed to wash off half the locations on it, the name of every island surrounding the big *X*, and even the compass in the corner, which was supposed to show him if he was holding it upside down or not (he was). In fact, the only piece of useful information that remained on the map was that the big *X* was somewhere near the Angerland Sea (which was, unfortunately for Vlad, the biggest of all the seven seas).

In actual fact, Vlad *had* found the exact location where *X* marked the spot a number of times – sixteen to be exact – but since his dad was never there, he always assumed he was in the wrong place. He also found lots of other interesting places in his search for his dad – the Puddle of Eternal Life, the Pothole of Never-Ending Gold, and, of course, the Island of

Unbelievably Cute and Fluffy Bunnies (but more on that later). None of these other discoveries ever interested Vlad though, because none of them gave him that warm, safe, comfortable feeling you get from being with someone who loves and understands you. So he just kept on searching. And, during his many years of searching, he managed to accrue a crew, and then a ship to put his crew on, and he eventually became one of the most feared pirates on the seven seas all because he was nice, and was forever trying to say nice things to people (which, of course, always came out as the *opposite* of nice). And that's how he ended up accidentally telling Ned to lock Harold and Ethel in his dungeon thing for the rest of their lives, (what he *thought* he had said was, "Go back and tell those lovely people that whenever they venture out on to these dangerous waters they will always have our protection. I grant them the freedom of the seven seas!"). Which brings us nicely back to what happened to them next...

THE DEEP, DARK, DUNGEONY DEPTHS OF VLAD'S VLADIATOR SHIP

The bright green parrot, who seemed to follow Sarah and Charlie everywhere they went, had made a brief visit to the *Vladiator*, to see how Harold and Ethel were doing. He was perched in a small, round downstairs window of the *Vladiator*, and he saw Harold and Ethel shivering behind bars, in the cold, dark, dungeony prison cell in the cold, dark belly of the *Vladiator*, and he wished there was something he could do to help them. Harold and Ethel were partly shivering from the cold, but mostly shivering in fear. Not in fear for themselves, though (Harold and Ethel were tough cookies. They had been through far worse things than a mere kidnapping!) – it was in fear for Sarah and Charlie, who they knew were now in grave danger.

"How have we let this happen, Harold?" Ethel whispered worriedly. "We've spent ten years doing everything in our power to protect Sarah and Charlie. We gave up our careers, our great big home, our fortune, our future ... and now it is all for nothing. We've been so busy making sure that Sarah and Charlie didn't get kidnapped that we've ended up getting kidnapped *ourselves*. And now they're out there, all alone, unprotected. We should have told them the truth from the very beginning! They have a right to know who we really are. About who *they* are."

"We decided not to tell them until they're grown-ups, Ethel, dear. Otherwise it could have put them in even more danger," Harold reminded her.

"But now we're going to die down here, all alone, and they will *never* discover the truth!"

"Ethel," Harold protested. "That's not true!"

"No?" said Ethel, doubtfully. "It's not? Which part isn't true?"

"The bit where you said we're all alone," Harold whispered.

Harold was right – they *weren't* alone... A door opened from upstairs. A shaft of light cut through the darkness. Harold and Ethel backed away from the bars of the dungeon as, very slowly, a pair of feet began clomping down the steps towards them.

The dark figure stepped forward into the light, revealing his face – it was Vladimir Death Pirate – and Ethel instantly rushed towards him, boiling with rage, clamouring to get through the bars that kept her from him.

"*You!*" she spat. "How dare you? How *DARE* you!"

"You?" Vlad replied, stumbling backwards in surprise.

Why would anyone lock these two lovely people up?! he wondered to himself in shock. *And WHO would*

lock these lovely people up?!

"We showed you nothing but kindness and generosity," barked Ethel, "and you repay us by kidnapping us and locking us away in your stinking ship?"

"Yes," Vlad replied (shaking his head no).

"Yes indeed, how dare you!" blustered Harold, pushing in front of Ethel. "I demand to speak to whoever is in charge!"

"*He* is in charge, Harold," Ethel lamented.

"Oh, I see ... then ... erm... Then what is your name, sir?" Harold demanded. "Tell me your name, and I shall report you to the authorities!"

Vlad couldn't speak for confusion, he just stood there, stammering.

"I ... I ... I..."

But Vlad didn't need to speak, because right there, among the many gold chains around his neck, hung a large, silver medal, with an inscription on it, which read *Vladimir Death Pirate – Second Most Dangerous Pirate on the Seven Seas.*

"No!" wailed Ethel, spotting the medal. "It's you! YOU! You're Vladimir Death Pirate?"

"What?" gasped Harold. "No!"

"It's him, Harold, *HIM*!" Ethel screamed and cried at the same time. "The pirate who killed our darling daughter!"

STOPPPPP!

I've only gone and ruined one of the biggest surprisey-monkeys in the story! (Surprisey-monkey is how all the cool kids in Angerland say "surprise", so I'm saying it too. Because I'm a fool. I mean cool.) Yes, yes, we all knew that something bad had happened to Sarah and Charlie's parents, and we knew that a pirate had something to do with it, but I wanted to keep the whole "Vlad killed them" thing to be a big "Gosh! Gasp! Surprisey-monkey!" kind of shock, for the next chapter. It was going to be brilliant! It was going to be so...

Wait.

I know.

I have an idea.

Try very hard to forget what you just read about Vlad being a killer.

Done? Forgotten?

No?

Do try harder then. Wipe it from existence. It never happened. You never read it. You are feeling verrrrry sleeeeeepy. Your eyes are getting verrrrrry heavyyyyyy. You want to give me lots of chocolaaaate. And when I click my fingers you will have forgotten everything I said about you know what.

Three.

Two.

One.

CLICK. (That was the sound of my fingers clicking.)

Well done! You have now successfully forgotten everything I ever said about Harold and Ethel's daughter being murdered by Vladimir Death Pi—

Drat. Drat. Drat!

Forget you read that last line. You are feeling verrrry sleeeepy...

A TOTALLY "GOSH! GASP! SURPRISEY-MONKEY!" KIND OF CHAPTER ALL ABOUT HOW HAROLD AND ETHEL'S DAUGHTER HAD BEEN MURDERED BY ~~VLADIMIR DEATH PIRATE~~ NOBODY. NO ONE. NOTHING TO SEE HERE. MOVE ALONG TO THE NEXT PARAGRAPH, PLEASE. GO. NOW. MOVE.

Way, way back, when Harold and Ethel's daughter was murdered, there had been an amazing discovery – they found out *who* had murdered her!

And that person was...

(Drum roll...)

It was...

(Nail chewing...)

It wasssss...

(Dum dum duuummmmmm!)

It was none other than...

(Wait for it…)

Vladimir Death Pirate!

GOSH!

GASP!

SURPRISEY-MONKEY!

I'LL
TRY THAT AGAIN,
BUT WITH A
BIT MORE DETAIL...

I know it might be hard to believe that kind-hearted, animal-loving Vlad could ever murder anyone, but the simple fact remained — sometimes, thanks to his opposite way of speaking, Vlad accidentally made bad things happen. This particular bad thing all began way, way back, two years and eighteen days before Sarah and Charlie were even born. Allow me to explain...

Two years and eighteen days before the day that Sarah and Charlie were born, things in Angerland were going along as usual – people were milling around, doing their day-to-day stuff, like ... I don't know, I wasn't really paying too much attention, to be honest, until...

Grimelda the Pure of Heart (yes, *that* Grimelda – the witch who gave Vlad his opposite speak; you know, the one who was famous for being OK at doing spells, but not so good with prophecies) appeared in the palace courtyard to announce her usual inaccurate and depressing Tuesday afternoon prophecies.

"A witch will appear in the palace courtyards today!" she had shouted, which had instantly got everyone's attention because, for once, her prediction was actually *true*. "And she will make an uncanny and depressing prophecy! Then she will disappear, never to be seen agaaaaiiiiiiiin!" The crowd gasped at the accuracy of this prophecy, and then, in a puff of smoke, the witch disappeared (actually she just scurried away and hid behind a water trough and whispered, "Pretend you can't see me!").

"Oooh! I almost forgot!" she continued, jumping back to her feet and running to the centre of the courtyard again. "And another thing ... on the night of their first child's birth, Princess Grunt, Prince Mellybottom and the rest of the royal family will disappear, never to be seen again!" She paused here while everybody laughed for five minutes and eleven seconds (not because they thought this news was funny, but because the witch had said "Prince Mellybottom" – *everyone* laughed when they heard his name, they couldn't help it!). And then everybody gasped in shock at the terrible prophecy, and the witch disappeared again. She had run out of puffs of smoke, so instead she hollered, "Everybody close your eyes! No peeking! Keep them closed until I say you can open them..." Everybody closed their eyes and listened to a noise that sounded a lot like a witch running away, and then, sounding as though she was far, far away, they heard her voice call again, "You can open your eyes now!" So everyone in the courtyard opened their eyes and gasped in amazement, for the witch had truly disappeared into thin air (or rather, the bakery).

From that day onwards everyone in Angerland feared what might happen if Princess Grunt and Prince Mellybottom ever had a baby. And then, two years and eighteen days later, Angerland was alive with celebration, dancing in the streets, fireworks in the sky, and lots of nervous mutterings about – "What if the prophecy was true?" For Princess Grunt and Prince Mellybottom had given birth to a child – *two* children, to be precise... Twins.

TWINS!

Do you see where this is going?! Have you made the connection yet? TWINS, I TELL YOU! BORN TEN YEARS AGO! *ROYAL TWINS!!!*

One was a boy, and the other was a girl, and they were named...

Sarah and Charlie.

Have you got it? Yes, *our* Sarah and Charlie! The very same Sarah and Charlie who grew up in a tiny cottage, in the woods, in the middle of nowhere, without a penny to their name. They had been a real-life prince and princess the whole time, and they never even knew it. And that was just *one* of the many secrets that Harold and Ethel had kept from the twins in an attempt to keep them hidden from Vladimir Death Pirate.

Sitting way up on a clifftop, looking out across the ocean as the sun went down, were two people who had slipped away from the festivities – Princess Grunt and Prince Mellybottom, Sarah and Charlie's mum and dad. They sat on a blanket on the grass, amongst a herd of gently grazing goats, and (surprise, surprise) a bright green parrot, and they celebrated by eating fish fingers and sipping sheepsnot (which wasn't actually the snot of sheep; it was the juice of apples. I'm not sure why they didn't just call it apple juice, actually), whilst, back at the palace, their newborn babies were having their first ever portraits painted, whilst being fussed over by their grandparents, Queen Ethel and King Harold.

It's not exactly usual for someone to go picnicking on a clifftop just hours after giving birth, but this

had not been a usual birth — it had been performed by the royal wizard, who had bypassed all the pain and discomfort of a normal birth by simply chanting, "Izzy wizzy, let's get those babies out of there!" then pulling the twins out of a hat that Princess Grunt held between her knees.

Princess Grunt now looked radiant. She was a picture of perfection. A glowing, mesmerizing beacon of beauty. She was ... well, actually, she was one of the ugliest people in the entire world, but that's not important. Who cares what she looked like? She was the mother of a perfect new baby or two, and she was in love, that's all that matters. Plus, for all I know she *may* have looked beautiful at this moment in time; it was hard to tell because the sun had gone down and it was so dark you couldn't have seen your hand if it were right in front of your face, or, in this case, if a goat's backside were right in front of your face.

"We did it." Princess Grunt beamed with delight at the inky black patch of air where she thought Prince Mellybottom was.

"We created an heir to the throne," she continued, sounding extremely happy. "We actually had a baby! No, not just one baby – twins! Can you believe it? We did it, Mellybottom!"

And then she laughed for five minutes and eleven seconds. (Yes, even *she* laughed whenever she heard that name.)

"The witch's prophecy was wrong all along!" she continued when she had finally finished laughing. "We *are* alive, and so are our beautiful little babies!"

"Yes, darling. To Sarah and Charlie!" cheered Mellybottom, raising a glass of sheepsnot.

"To Sarah and Charlie!" agreed Princess Grunt.

So, they gulped down their sheepsnot, and then leaned in for a deeply romantic kiss.

But as Prince Mellybottom puckered up and lunged in, he couldn't help notice that Princess Grunt's face felt a little bit ... *hairy*. And her breath smelled a little bit ... *bottomy*. And her lips felt a teensy bit ... *goaty*. This may have had something to do with the fact that Princess Grunt was actually sitting half an elephant to Mellybottom's left, and the hairy, bottomy, goaty thing that Mellybottom was giving a sloppy great kiss was in actual fact...

A hairy goat's bottom.

One lesson you should take away from this horrific event is this – never kiss a goat's bottom on a clifftop. If you choose not to take this advice, and you do go kissing a goat's bottom on a clifftop, you can expect three things to happen:

1. The goat will, most probably, fart with surprise.
2. The goat will kick.
3. You will fall straight over the edge of the cliff.

Which is exactly what happened to Princess Grunt and Prince Mellybottom. And that is how Grimelda's prophecy came true, and they were never seen again.

Unfortunately for Vlad, his ship had been spotted near Angerland earlier that day, so, naturally, he got the blame for Grunt and Mellybottom's tragic disappearance. Vlad quickly made a public announcement to explain his innocence, but thanks to his opposite speak, it didn't quite work.

"I, Vladimir Death Pirate, know exactly what happened to Princess Grunt and Prince Mellybottom," Vlad adamantly proclaimed. "I killed them. Because I'm horrible. And I intend to do the same to the rest of the royal family."

And that's when Harold and Ethel decided to take baby Sarah and baby Charlie to live in hiding, in the woods, and spend the next ten years preparing them for the day when Vladimir Death Pirate would eventually find them – showing them how to survive, training them for the unknown, teaching them how to avoid certain death.

Unfortunately, though, "certain death" was exactly where Sarah and Charlie were now heading.

SARAH'S RESCUE PLAN

The bright green parrot caught up with Sarah and Charlie as they were racing through the woods, hot on the trail of Harold and Ethel and the pirates who'd stolen them. Thankfully the pirates had left a very clear trail of footprints, litter and trampled foliage – it looked like a herd of elephant-sized donkeys had passed through the woods.

"So . . . what do we do when we actually catch up with them?" Charlie panted fearfully.

"Simple," Sarah said, with a knowing smile, "we give the call of the SSP."

"The Secret Sea Police!" Charlie gasped in awe, so excited that he completely stopped running.

The Secret Sea Police were heroes to Charlie. They were heroes to *everyone*. Well, everyone except pirates. The Secret Sea Police had one job, and one job only – to get rid of every single pirate on the seven seas. They were the bravest of the brave, the strongest of the strong, they came face-to-face with danger every day, and they never, ever backed away from a challenge. No matter how big or how small a pirate ship might be, it was the duty of the Secret Sea Police to destroy that ship, as fast and effectively as possible. In short, they were unstoppable destroyers of all things piratical.

"What do you do if you ever find yourself out at sea, in the company of a pirate?" Grandma Ethel would quiz Sarah and Charlie on a regular basis.

"We call the Secret Sea Police," Sarah and Charlie would groan in unison.

"And how do you call the Secret Sea Police?"

"You tip your head back, you open your mouth as wide as you can, then you scream the words

PICAROON OBLITERATE FILIBUSTER DECIMATE PILLAGER ERADICATE BEASTLY BANDIT BOOM!

Then the Secret Sea Police turn up and catch any pirates in the area," they told her every time.

"Yes! We'll call the Secret Sea Police! That's a genius plan, Sarah!" Charlie enthused as he began running again, further towards the sea than he and Sarah had ever dared go on their own before. "We get the adventure of *hunting* the pirates, with none of the dangers of *fighting* them! Plus I might even get to meet Tenacious Hunt!"

Tenacious Hunt was the commander of the Secret Sea Police, and Charlie's all-time hero. The thought of actually meeting him filled Charlie with a tingly sense of giddiness, but then that tingly sensation suddenly disappeared and was replaced by a soggy, heavy, dull worry.

"What is it?" asked Sarah, noticing the serious look on Charlie's face.

"How can I look Tenacious Hunt in the eye when he's so heroic and I'm so ... you know, *not* heroic. I'm fed up of being rubbish at everything, Sarah. I want to be amazing, like Tenacious Hunt! I want to help," Charlie said, sounding determined but looking a bit sad. "I mean I *properly* want to help. And I want to prove to Grandma and Grandpa that I *can* do things – that I'm not the little baby they think I am."

Sarah raised her eyebrows sceptically.

"You can do anything you put your mind to, Charlie, I'm sure of it," Sarah told him; then she turned to run the last few elephants to where the woods ended and the beach began. (Please don't

71

forget that elephants are a measurement or you'll get really confused.)

As they carefully stepped out from amongst the trees and on to a deserted, sandy beach where the waves gently lapped the shore, they paused again in amazement at the sheer magnitude of the vast blue shark-infested ocean (they had only ever seen it twice before, and only ever through Grandpa Harold's telescope, whilst they were safely hidden away in the trees).

Charlie gasped as he spotted a gigantic, distant shadow-like object disappear around the corner of the bay.

"There they are!" he exclaimed. "A pirate ship! It's them, Sarah, it has to be them! Let's follow it!"

But Sarah didn't move.

She just stood there with a horrified look on her face.

"Oh dear," she said, numbly.

"What?" asked Charlie.

"We have a problem."

"What is it? Maybe I could put my mind to it and sort it out!"

"I don't think so," Sarah said grimly. "Not this time."

"Why? What is it?"

"Just a tiny detail..."

"Yes?"

"That could ruin all our plans..."

"What!"

"We ... kind of ... erm ... forgot the boat."

Charlie's mouth slowly dropped open.

"Oh dear," he said.

"And our swords," added Sarah.

"Oh dear," said Charlie.

"And our compasses, matches, waterproofs and drinks."

"Oh dear," repeated Charlie. "Did we bring *anything* useful?"

"I brought a telescope and some biscuits. What about you?"

"Mr Cuddles."

"You brought your toy hedgehog?"

"Seemed like a good idea at the time." Charlie shrugged innocently.

"Oh dear," said Sarah.

"What are you ... I mean, what are *we* going to do?" asked Charlie, trying not to sound too scared.

"I don't know what we *can* do," Sarah said gravely. "It'll take *hours* if we go back to get the boat. We'd have no chance of ever catching up with the pirates!"

"But we'll have even less chance of catching them *without* a boat," reasoned Charlie.

Sarah slumped into the sand and hung her head in her hands.

"We haven't even started our first ever adventure and we've already failed," she groaned with shame. "We're never going to find them!"

And then Sarah and Charlie heard a noise that made their hearts scream in panic.

"Well, we could use *mine*, I suppose," said a voice from behind them.

Sarah and Charlie leapt into the air, then spun around to see who was behind them.

As if being so close to the dreaded sea wasn't scary enough, they now found themselves face-to-face with the only other thing they had always been taught to stay away from – a *stranger*.

THE STRANGER

The stranger stepped out from amongst the trees with a huge grin spread across his face and a long, greasy fringe obscuring his eyes.

The parrot gave a squawk of surprise and shot into the air as Sarah and Charlie stumbled backwards, away from the stranger, the whole time edging closer and closer to the dreaded sea.

"Who are you?" Sarah demanded, her voice trembling with fright. "What do you want?"

"My name is ... well, let's not worry ourselves

about that," said the stranger, shifting awkwardly on the spot. "The important thing is that you two need a boat, and I just so happen to have two spare seats in mine. Come on, I'll show you."

The stranger didn't hang around to chat. He simply turned and walked off down the beach.

Sarah looked at Charlie.

Charlie looked at Sarah.

Neither of them knew what to do!

And then Sarah made a decision – she began following the stranger. Charlie followed close behind. They made sure to keep their distance, and Sarah picked up a big, spiky branch from the edge of the woods. It wasn't as good as a sword, but it would have to do. She hated to think what Harold and Ethel would say if they ever found out that they were by the *sea* without their *swords*, and with a *stranger*!

As they approached the stranger's boat, something started to feel wrong to Sarah. Maybe it was because the stranger wasn't talking. Maybe it was just because they had never been alone with anyone who wasn't family before. Or maybe it was because the stranger's boat was in fact a bathtub.

Whatever the reason, Sarah didn't like it, and she found herself gripping on to that spiky branch for dear life.

"This isn't a boat," Sarah pointed out, unimpressed.

"That's right," the stranger agreed enthusiastically. "It's so much more than just a boat – it's a boat *and* a bathtub all in one!"

"What's the point in that?" asked Charlie.

"Well, you can have a bath while you're sailing," said the stranger, with an "obviously!" kind of shrug.

"But ... wouldn't the bath *sink* if you filled it with water?" said Charlie.

"Well, err ... I don't think there will be room for your weird parrot," said the stranger, quickly changing the subject.

"He's not *our* weird parrot," Sarah stated. "He's just a random parrot who follows us round. Plus, I don't think we can really stop him tagging along since he can, you know, *fly.*"

"Well, I suppose," agreed the stranger, "but there's something about him that's just a bit ... weird."

"Says the man with a bathtub for a boat!" Charlie muttered under his breath.

"Why are you so desperate for a boat anyway?" enquired the stranger as he began dragging the bathtub to the water's edge.

"Our grandparents have been kidnapped by pirates, and we're going to get them back," said Charlie, before Sarah had finished deciding whether or not to tell the stranger the truth.

"You mean that big pirate ship that just disappeared around the corner?"

"Yes!"

"Well, we better hurry up, then! Come on, in you get!"

And before Sarah had finished deciding whether

or not it was a good idea to get in the stranger's bath boat, she found she was already in it.

They slid out into deeper waters, trying to keep up with the pirate ship ahead of them, which kept slipping in and out of view as it rounded the cove. Sarah looked out at the vast and daunting ocean, then at the many shark fins that were circling their boat, and then, finally, at the strange man whose boat they were now in, and Sarah began to worry that they had made a very bad move.

He might not be a baddie, Sarah reassured herself, *and even if he is, me and Charlie have been training to protect ourselves against people like him our entire lives! We can run! We can hide! We can sword fight!*

And then Sarah realized the three horrifyingly big problems with that plan:

1. There is nowhere to run when you're surrounded by sharks.
2. There is nowhere to hide when you're stuck in a bathtub.

3. There is no way to sword fight when your sword is at home, under your bed.

Sarah clutched that spiky branch so tightly that her knuckles turned white. She couldn't believe how stupid she had been! They were out at SEA, with a STRANGER, surrounded by SHARKS, and there was no way of escaping! Nowhere to hide! No way of...

Sarah's train of thought was completely broken when the stranger turned to her and grinned a long, unnerving grin.

Eventually the stranger spoke. And when he did, it made shivers run down Sarah's spine.

"How rude of me," he said, in an unnaturally soft voice, still smiling from ear to ear. "I haven't made my introductions."

He stared at the children for an uncomfortably long time, then got to his feet and said: "Allow me to introduce you ... *to* **CERTAIN DEATH!**"

FACE-TO-FACE WITH CERTAIN DEATH

Now then, where was I? I think I had been about to tell you about Harold's collection of pickled carrots that were all shaped like... No! Ah! Yes! The stranger was about to introduce Sarah and Charlie to certain death!

Certain death?

CERTAIN DEATH!

Charlie and Sarah suddenly began to panic more than they had ever panicked in their lives! It was a panic of *epic proportions*! (Well, maybe not *epic* proportions, probably more like a panic of really quite big, maybe large, or extra-large proportions. Definitely bigger than medium, but smaller than huge. Anyway...) They were trapped in a floating bathtub, in the middle of a shark-infested ocean, with a man who wanted to kill them, and there was no escape.

Sarah decided it was time to take her grandparents' advice – so, without wasting a single second, she tipped her head back, opened her mouth as wide as she could, then, at the top of her voice, screamed these words:

PICAROON OBLITERATE FILIBUSTER DECIMATE PILLAGER ERADICATE BEASTLY BANDIT BOOM!

The smile fell from the stranger's face. His skin turned a greenish grey colour. And he suddenly looked extremely scared.

"Surprisey-monkey," snarled Sarah. "The Secret Sea Police are coming to get you!"

This was the most awesome thing Sarah had ever done. She felt invincible. She felt unstoppable. She felt the coolest she had ever been in her life.

"Erm ... sorry," said the stranger, "but you do know that *Certain Death* is the name of my boat, right?"

Suddenly Sarah didn't feel quite so cool any more.

"W ... what?" she stammered, now taking *her* turn to go a greeny-greyish colour.

"My boat. That's who I was about to introduce you to! I named it *Certain Death: Queen of the Ocean.*"

"Errrrm ... he's telling the truth," said Charlie, pointing to the side of the bathtub, where there hung a scruffy sign that looked as though a child had painted it. Sarah leaned across Charlie and read the sign.

"Certain Death: Queen of the O ... oh ... OH NO!"

Sarah had leaned too far over. The bathtub tipped, and she was plunged, head first, into the shark-infested waters!

Huge grey fins instantly stopped circling and darted towards her with horrifying speed. Sarah tried to pull herself back into the tub, but the sides were too high. She looked down into the water and saw a set of gigantic, razor-toothed jaws rising up beneath her, then – *SPLOOOSH!* Sarah was back in the bathtub, safe in the arms of the stranger as the shark shot out of the water, gnashing its teeth on nothing but air.

"You saved me!" Sarah spluttered, trembling with shock.

"Of course I saved you!" The stranger laughed weakly, trembling almost as much as Sarah. "I wouldn't let anything happen to you!"

And Sarah could hear in his voice that he meant it. He meant it like Sarah meant that she would never let anything happen to her grandma and grandpa, like...

"Grandma and Grandpa!" Sarah gasped, bolting up in horror. "Where are they?"

She got to her feet and looked in every direction, but the pirate ship they had been following was nowhere to be seen.

"They've gone! We've lost them! I was so busy worrying about *us* that I forgot about *them*!"

"Nooo!" Charlie groaned as he too got to his feet and scanned the horizon for any sign of the pirate ship

"They can't have gone far," the stranger assured them.

"But we don't even know what direction they went in!" Sarah shrieked in panic. "They could have gone *anywhere*!"

"Well, they were heading east," the stranger told them in a calm and reassuring voice. "So if we keep heading in that direction, we're bound to spot them eventually."

"Really?" asked Sarah, half hopeful, half sceptical.

"Really," the stranger assured her. Then he hoisted the mainsail and the bathtub suddenly picked up speed. "We'll catch up with them in no time."

"Thank you," said Sarah, finally warming to the stranger as she and Charlie sat themselves back down, disappointed but not disheartened. "And sorry about the whole Secret Sea Police thing."

"Don't worry about it, Miss ... erm...?"

"Sarah," said Sarah, shaking the stranger's hand. "And this is my brother, Charlie."

"So ... so you're not a bad guy then?" asked Charlie as he took his turn to shake hands with the stranger.

"No, Chesney, I'm not a bad guy," said the stranger, smiling as he ruffled Charlie's hair. "You and Sybil have absolutely nothing to worry about."

"My name's actually Sarah," Sarah quietly corrected him.

"And my name's not Chesney, it's Charlie," Charlie added.

"It's a pleasure to have you on board my ship, Zara and Chris. My name is . . . my name is . . . well, I don't actually remember what my name is. Let's just say I'm called . . . Bingo. No, not Bingo, that's a rubbish name. How about . . . Bartholomew. No, no, too long. I need something a bit more menacing, a bit more *grrrrrrrr*, a name that will strike fear into the hearts of my enemies, a name like. . ." The stranger paused, and his eyes instantly widened as the most perfect, blood-curdling, spine-chilling name suddenly popped into his head.

"Yes?" Sarah urged him eagerly, from the edge of her seat.

The stranger leaned forward, lowered his voice, mustered all his courage, and finally managed to whisper the horrifying name. . .

"Captain *Honk*."

Sarah and Charlie stared at him with unimpressed blankness.

"I know," Honk nodded, smugly. "Prettttty scary, right?"

Sarah and Charlie struggled to stifle their laughter.

"Sorry," said Sarah, trying to disguise her snorts of amusement as a coughing fit, "but why would the name *Captain Honk. . .*"

"AAAARGHHH! SORRY," Honk screamed at the very sound of his new name. "Carry on."

"Why would the name *Captain Honk. . .*"

"AAAARGHHH! SORRY," Honk screamed again.

"Why would . . . *that name* strike fear into the hearts of your enemies?" Sarah finally managed to ask.

"It strikes fear into *my* heart!" explained Honk.

"Really? I'd never have guessed," Charlie muttered quietly.

"Well, let me explain. You see, it all goes way, way back to . . . nope, sorry, I don't remember. All I can remember is that it was dark, I was scared, there was a loud HONKing sound, then there was an awful, pungent odour, and that's when *this* happened. . ."

Honk lifted his floppy fringe to reveal a huge dent in the side of his head.

"Oh my goodness!" gasped Sarah, recoiling in disgust.

"And then it all goes blank. I don't remember anything past that point," explained Honk, knocking the dent with his knuckles.

"You don't remember *anything*?" asked Charlie.

"Nope," confirmed Honk.

"Nothing?" asked Sarah.

"Nothing apart from that terrible smell and that awful sound. I don't remember who I am, where I lived, who my parents were ... you're lucky I've even managed to remember your names!"

Sarah and Charlie decided not to comment on this.

"So, what made you decide to start sailing around in a bathtub then?" asked Charlie.

"Well, Chuck, that I *do* remember – I am on a quest! I'm searching for..."

"Let me guess," groaned Sarah, "you're

searching for the Island of Unbelievably Cute and Fluffy Bunnies, so that you can go to the magical meadow at its centre and make your one wish, to get your memory back?"

"How did you know!" Honk gasped in amazement.

"I haven't met a single person who *isn't* searching for it," explained Sarah. (And since the only other people she had ever met were Harold and Ethel, she wasn't even exaggerating!)

"I don't suppose I'll be finding it anytime soon anyway," Honk said wistfully.

"Why not?" Charlie asked.

"Well, because we'll all be dead by the end of the day!" Honk exclaimed as if this was old news.

"We'll all be ... *what?*" gasped Sarah, looking both confused and concerned.

"Dead. The Secret Sea Police will turn up, blow us all to smithereens, and we'll be turned into little blobs of fish food. You know how it is," Honk said with a sigh.

"Well, I'm sure the Secret Sea Police will realize that it was an honest misunderstanding. I'll just explain it to them. It'll be fine," Sarah reassured him.

"I'm afraid it's not quite that simple," said Captain Honk, shaking his head sadly. "You see, the Secret Sea Police don't stop to make conversation. When they find a pirate ship, they destroy it, along with everyone on board."

"Then we don't have anything to worry about!" said Charlie, cheerfully. "They only attack pirate ships, and this isn't a pirate ship!"

"Ah," said the stranger. "About that ... you may want to look up."

Sarah and Charlie both looked up, and there, flapping in the wind above them at the top of a mast, was not the usual red flag displayed by your average, innocent seafaring folk, but a big black flag with a white skull and crossbones painted on it, along with the words "Pie Rat".

Sarah and Charlie both gulped in fear.

"You're ... you're a *pirate*?" Sarah stuttered.

"'Fraid so," said Honk, with an apologetic shrug. "I predict we have about four and a half minutes before we're torn to pieces by their cannonballs."

"Oh dear," said Charlie.

"Yes," muttered Sarah. "Oh dear."

"I agree," said Honk. "Oh − and very much − dear."

"Squawk!" agreed the bright green parrot, who decided that this might be a good opportunity to pay Harold and Ethel a visit, and flew off in the direction of the *Vladiator*.

Calling the Secret Sea Police was the worst mistake in the entire history of bad mistakes. OK, maybe not in the *entire* history of bad mistakes, but at least since the day, way, way back, when the royal wizard of Angerland accidentally turned himself into a bright green parrot.

WAY, WAY BACK, WHEN THE ROYAL WIZARD ACCIDENTALLY TURNED HIMSELF INTO A BRIGHT GREEN PARROT

Yes, it's true, a long time ago the cleverest, most talented wizard in the history of Angerland accidentally turned himself into a parrot. Actually, that's not entirely correct — he had turned himself into a parrot *on purpose*; the accident had been that he had no idea how to turn himself *back* again.

The trouble all began on the day that Sarah and Charlie were born.

Worried that the witch's prophecy could be correct, and that members of the royal family might disappear, Ethel had asked the royal wizard to keep a watchful eye over Princess Grunt the entire day that she gave birth to the twins. So that was what the royal wizard did. In fact, he went one better than that. Since it was the whole family that was in danger of disappearing, he kept a watchful eye on them *all*, and he did this by magically transforming himself into a parrot so he could fly back and forth between each member of the family, at great speed. He had never turned himself into an animal before, and was a little worried it could go wrong, but the spell was a complete success. All it took was for the royal wizard to read a few lines from a book, do a flick of his wrist, and hey presto – he was a parrot. Turning himself back should have been just as simple, except for one little detail – he had not turned himself into one of those clever *talking* parrots, which meant he couldn't speak, which meant he had no way of saying the spell that would turn him back into a human. He hadn't even told anyone what his plan was, so not a single person knew that he was the parrot! And without a voice he had no way of ever explaining the situation to them. So that's how he remained for years to come – a genius, trapped in the body of a birdbrain.

One minute he was the world's greatest wizard, ready to assist the royal family in any task, at any time. And the next minute he was a good-for-nothing, useless little parrot. The only thing he now had any talent for was spying on people, and learning the secret stories of everyone he met – stories that he would commit to memory, and later turn into a book, a rather fantastic book, about pirates, princesses, witches and, most importantly, a bright green parrot (you should read it sometime! page 96 is especially good).

Yes, that book is *this* book. And yes, that parrot is the *narrator* of this book. That parrot is *me* – Sebillius Quark, royal wizard extraordinaire, and not very good teller of stories. Ten long years I had been stuck being a parrot, unable to do anything to assist the royal family, but then came a day – the day of this story – when the royal family needed my help more than ever before.

I had to find a way of turning myself back into a wizard.

I had to help them.

Failure was not an option because, as you will discover in the next chapter, things were about to get *very* bad indeed.

THINGS GET
VERY BAD INDEED

The astoundingly clever, exceedingly talented, and stunningly handsome parrot arrived at the *Vladiator* and flew down... No, hang on, sorry, I mean *I* arrived at the *Vladiator*, flew down around the outside of the big black ship, and peered in through the window of the dungeon to see Ethel and Harold, trembling uncontrollably in the face of their ultimate nemesis – Vladimir Death Pirate. But there was no longer any *fear* mixed into their trembling; this time it was pure, undiluted *anger*. I hated to see them so upset. A royal wizard could have set them free with one brief spell, but being a stupid parrot, there was nothing I could do except watch events unfold, feeling helpless and useless and pathetic and rubbish and a little bit not great.

"I want you to answer me just one question, you monster," Ethel growled as she clutched the wooden bars that stood between her and Vlad.

"*One* question," echoed Harold.

"Did you murder our daughter?" Ethel boldly asked.

"*Did* you?" echoed Harold.

"Yes," Vlad replied nervously.

At first Ethel did nothing. She simply stared into Vlad's eyes. And then, as quick as a flash, she darted towards the small round window in the side wall of their dungeony prison thing. She shoved the beautiful bright green me out of her way, then she threw her head back, opened her mouth as wide as she could, and screamed these words...

PICAROON OBLITERATE FILIBUSTER DECIMATE PILLAGER ERADICATE BEASTLY BANDIT BOOM!

"Boom!" Harold feebly added, for a little extra support.

Vlad stumbled backwards in fear.

"You'd better be afraid," hissed Ethel, turning on him.

"Be *jolly* afraid," Harold whispered, trying (and failing) to seem menacing.

"The Secret Sea Police are coming to get you," continued Ethel. "And when they capture you, I will personally make sure that they chop you up into little pieces and feed you to the sharks!"

"And the *beavers*," hissed Harold.

"I'm not scared," said Vlad who was actually the *opposite* of not scared. "And I'm not sorry!" (Except he was. He really, *really* was. Sorry for the whole gigantic misunderstanding.)

"The Secret Sea Police will *make* you sorry!" Ethel roared. "That's if I don't get you first!"

Ethel leapt towards Vlad, grabbed hold of the thick bamboo bars of the dungeon, and then did something that Vlad could barely believe – she began *chewing* through them! (Super strong teeth are one of the many benefits of having a royal wizard do your dental work for most of your life.) And then Harold joined in too.

"When we escape from here I'm going to use these teeth to make you sorry you ever came anywhere near my family!" Ethel shrieked like a madwoman. "When I've bitten through these bars I'll bite through your fingers, and when I've bitten through your fingers I'll bite through your toes, and when I've bitten through your toes I'll bite your entire head off!"

"And I'll bite your *bottom!*" added Harold, which sounded a bit weirder than he'd intended.

Vlad backed away. He stumbled, then fell, then scrambled to his feet, and began to run. He had seen in Ethel's eyes that she had meant every word. So Vlad ran. He ran for his life.

The bright green ... I mean, *I* couldn't take it any longer; it was time to put an end to being a useless yet very good-looking parrot. I *had* to do something! I had to help Harold and Ethel get back to Sarah and Charlie! I had to save poor, misunderstood Vlad from having his fingers, toes, face and bottom eaten off! And I had to save *everyone* from being destroyed by the Secret Sea Police, who were surely on their way by now!

But I still had the problem of not being able to talk in order to cast my spells. However, I'd heard about magicians in ancient times being able to cast spells by just *thinking* the words, instead of saying them out loud, so I screwed up all my courage and decided to give it a go. Never mind the four hundred and eight times I'd tried before and been unsuccessful. This time I *had* to make it work! All I had to do was to close my eyes, raise my right arm (hopefully a wing would do), turn in a counter-clockwise circle, and think the word "undo" very clearly.

Theoretically this should undo the spell that turned me into the very handsome (but not very helpful) parrot that I had become.

I closed my eyes.

I focused all my energy.

Then I raised my handsome right wing.

Turned in a circle.

Said the word "undo!" over and over again in my mind.

And then...

POP!

Something happened!

I opened my eyes...

Golden sparkles rained down around me...

Magic was definitely in the air!

A spell had been cast!

I peered into the dungeon.

And to my amazement I saw...

Harold and Ethel's hair had grown down to their knees.

The only thing I had managed to "undo" was every haircut Harold and Ethel had ever had.

I was officially useless. And still just a parrot.

All I could hope for now was that a) Harold and Ethel didn't manage to eat through those bars (for Vlad's sake), and that b) the Secret Sea Police somehow didn't receive those messages.

But then, all of a sudden, two things happened.

1. Harold and Ethel *did* eat through those bars.

2. The next chapter came along.

THE ISLAND OF THE
SECRET SEA POLICE

In the great dark ocean, beneath a great dark cloud, sat a great dark island. And on that great dark island was a great dark cave, and in that great dark cave sat the friendly little receptionist for the Secret Sea Police, with beautiful long legs, delightfully curly blonde hair, and a jaw that worked tirelessly on a stick of chewing gum. His name was Frank, today was his fifty-fourth birthday, and he was bored out of his mind. Frank wasn't always this bored – he usually *loved* his job – but it had been a slow few months for the Secret Sea Police, and everyone was anxious for the next case to arrive. Frank was just about to begin his third tea break of the morning when something caused him to freeze on the spot.

An eerie, echoing voice magically drifted into the cave like the ghost of a young, distant damsel in distress. "PICAROON OBLITERATE FILIBUSTER DECIMATE PILLAGER ERADICATE BEASTLY BANDIT – BOOM," the voice echoed.

Frank's teacup dropped to the floor with a *SMASH* as he dashed to the emergency conch to relay the message to the officers in the upper caves.

"Emergency call!" he yelled into the conch. "I repeat – we have an emergency call!"

And then a second call came magically drifting into the cave, like the ghost of a rather old, slightly royal lady in distress.

"Correction!" Frank yelled, picking up the conch again. "*Two* emergency calls! I repeat – *TWO* calls!!"

Forty-seven seconds later, the Secret Sea Police's

boat, the SSP *Destroyer*, sped down its deployment ramp, slipped silently into the great dark sea, then raced away on its mighty mission. For the first time in months, the Secret Sea Police were about to do what they were born to do – destroy pirates.

Yes, the heroic Secret Sea Police were on their way! This was a good day! This was a momentous occasion! This was … bad news for anyone who happened to be in a pirate ship.

GET VLAD!

Back in the dungeon of the *Vladiator*, Vlad was scared out of his wits. Not only were the Secret Sea Police on their way to destroy him along with his boat and all chances of him ever finding his dad at the *X* on his map – but there were also two crazy old people threatening to eat his bottom off! And he didn't even know why! He didn't even know how they had got there! He'd told his crew to offer them the freedom of the seven seas, and now they were on his boat, accusing him of murdering their daughter. Vlad didn't have a clue what was going on. He scrambled away from them as fast as he could, and raced back towards the stairs.

"First Mate Ned?" Vlad wailed.

"Cap'n?" came the nervous voice of Ned from the room at the top of the stairs.

"The Secret Sea Police are not on their way! And nobody is trying to eat my head!"

"That's nice, Cap'n," Ned replied. "You just stay down there then." Ned was used to Vlad yelling pointless drivel at him from time to time, but unfortunately he wasn't quite clever enough to work out that Vlad always said the opposite of what he wanted to.

Harold and Ethel were squeezing themselves through the gap they had chewed between the bars, and were soon hot on the heels of the man they hated with every drop of hate in their hate-filled bodies.

With squeals of panic, Vlad frantically fled up the stairs and into Ned's room. He slammed the door shut behind him, locked it, and then collapsed on the floor in a fit of terror.

"You are such a genius!" he roared angrily at Ned. "I asked you not to help! I almost didn't die down there!"

"That's nice, Cap'n," Ned replied, a little confused by Vlad's anger at this good news.

BAM!

The door behind Vlad bulged as Harold and Ethel threw themselves at it from the other side.

"Again!" came Ethel's voice as they took a second run-up.

BAM!

"Harder!"

BAM!

They were determined to break through it. They knew they could do it. They knew that vengeance would soon be theirs. They knew that the Secret Sea Police were on their way! And they knew that Vlad would finally pay for his crime.

But of course, what they *didn't* know was that

Vlad *wasn't* Princess Grunt's killer. They *didn't* know that he had only admitted to the crime because he always said the opposite of what he wanted to say, without even realizing it.

They *didn't* know that every bad thing Vlad had ever done had all just been a series of huge misunderstandings, like, for instance, the awful thing that happened, way, way back, on the Island of Unbelievably Cute and Fluffy Bunnies.

It was awful.

You may want to read this next chapter with your eyes closed...

THE AWFUL THING THAT HAPPENED, WAY, WAY BACK, ON THE ISLAND OF UNBELIEVABLY CUTE AND FLUFFY BUNNIES

The sun was shining, the flowers were blooming, and on the Island of Unbelievably Cute and Fluffy Bunnies, there was, unsurprisingly, an abundance of unbelievably cute and fluffy bunnies hopping around and nibbling carrots. Spring was well and truly in the air.

And then the *Vladiator* arrived. The bunnies, in their naive and innocent bunny-like manner, rushed to greet the pirate visitors, and before long, the *Vladiator* was bouncing with beautiful life as hundreds of unbelievably cute and fluffy bunnies hopped on board and scampered playfully around.

"So, sir, what should we do with all of these unbelievably cute and fluffy bunnies?" asked First Mate Ned, when it was time to leave.

Vlad *thought* that he had replied: "Why, we should pepper them with kisses and cuddles, shower them with our love and affection, feed them our finest carrots, dress them in our most luxuriant bunny-sized frocks, teach them to dance around the maypole, then deposit them safely back on their island and leave them on their merry way as we set sail on these dark and dreary seas once more."

But what he had *actually* said was *this*: "Sit on them all, until they're SQUISHETY-SQUASH-SQUISHED!" Then he disappeared into his office to paint some pictures of puppies and kittens. And when all the bunnies were squished, they set sail.

Vlad didn't realize that all the bunnies were squished. He didn't even realize that he had stumbled upon a place that people had been searching for for hundreds of years, and he had absolutely no idea that he had just sailed away from the one place in the world that had the power to make his only wish come true — to see his dad again and feel that warm feeling of being loved and understood.

TRAPPED IN
A PIRATE BATHTUB

The tub of *Certain Death* ploughed purposefully along, with the cool ocean beneath it and the warm sunshine beating down from above as Sarah, Charlie and Honk continued their attempt to find the lost pirate ship. And, as they searched, the three of them finished off Sarah's biscuits and then fed the crumbs to a passing dolphin. Eager as they were to find Harold and Ethel, they decided that, if they really were going to be blown to pieces by the Secret Sea Police, then they may as well try to enjoy their last day on earth.

"So, are you *really* a pirate, Captain Honk?" asked Charlie as he patted the dolphin on the head.

"AAAARGHHH!" Honk screamed at the mention of his name. "Sorry. Well, I'm trying to be," he said, shrugging bashfully.

"Why would anyone *try* to be a pirate?" Charlie asked, crinkling his nose with disapproval.

"Why would I want to be a pirate?!" Honk laughed incredulously. (No, I don't know what "incredulously" means either, but I've seen it written in other books, so I thought I better try to fit it somewhere in this one too, just so people take it seriously.) "Pirates are the greatest people in the world! Pirates are brave! Pirates are exciting! Pirates are the only reason I started sailing in the first place!"

"Really?" Sarah asked with an incredulous curl of her lip. (Trust me, "incredulous" is what real storytellers say all the time. It's clever.) "I always thought pirates were dirty, stinking, thieving, cowardly, murderous criminals who are the scum of the earth."

"And ... well..." Honk sighed as he stared off into the water, almost as if he hadn't heard anything Sarah had said. "It also means I get to *be* somebody. I get to be a pirate instead of just a nobody. And that's quite important for someone who doesn't even know who he is."

Honk continued to sit, staring into the water, in silence, for a very long time. Sarah began to feel bad for what she'd said about pirates being the scum of the earth, and she worried that she might have been a little too offensive, especially considering that he had just saved her life. Honk stared, and he stared, and he stared, without saying another word, and if he had stared for just two seconds longer he would have broken the world record for Staring for a Really, Really Long Time, Without Blinking.

"Are you ... OK?" Sarah asked eventually.

"Sorry," Honk said to Sarah, "did you say something? I was *elephants* away, wondering why one earth we call lemons *lemons*. Why don't we call them *yellows*? I mean, oranges are called *orange*s! And surely limes should be called *greens*? And pink grapefruit – why bother with the 'grapefruit' bit? We already have a grape fruit – they're called *grapes*! Why can't pink grapefruit just be called *pinks*? Yes, pink…" Honk trailed off and his eyes glazed over as if remembering a long-lost love. "Hmmm, pink, like Captain Doom's ship."

"Yeah … erm … right. Pink," said Charlie as he and Sarah exchanged a look of complete and utter mind-boggling confuddlement. "If you say so. Pink, yeah, like Captain Doom's… Who's *Captain Doom*?"

"*Who's Captain Doom?!*" Honk gasped incredulously. "He's only the Number One Most Dangerous Pirate on the Seven Seas! Although actually he's not officially a pirate, he's a scavenger."

"Is he the one who killed that prince and princess, years ago?" asked Sarah.

"No, no, no, that's Vladimir Death Pirate; he's only the Second Most Dangerous Pirate on the Seven Seas. Captain Doom's *far* more dangerous."

"Why, what's so bad about him?" asked Sarah.

"What's so bad about him?! He's a ruthless force of destruction, that's what's so bad about him!" Honk whispered anxiously, as if just talking about him could get him into extremely incredulous trouble. "He's not like any other pirate that ever existed – he doesn't steal loot (unless it's from pirates), he doesn't kidnap people (unless they're pirates), and he doesn't – stop – sailing. *Ever!* Not even for supplies! He just destroys everything that gets in his way, and then scavenges everything he needs from the wreckages as they drift by."

"How come he never stops sailing?" asked Sarah, wondering how that could even be possible.

"Because he's obsessed. *Completely* obsessed! Obsessed with finding just one thing. And he won't stop sailing until he has found it. And do you want to know what that one thing is...?"

"The Island of Unbelievably Cute and Fluffy Bunnies," Sarah and Charlie both groaned together.

"Oh, how did you guess?" Honk asked, disappointed that his surprise had been ruined.

"*Everyone* seems to be looking for this island, even our *grandparents*, and they're quite intelligent people! But it doesn't make sense to me why *so* many people are searching for a place that so obviously doesn't *exist*!" Sarah scoffed.

"That doesn't ... that *doesn't exist*?" Honk repeated, with so much incredulosity that he began to turn red. "Why would you ever say such a thing?!"

"Because the entire world has been searching for it since *for ever*, but I've never heard of anyone finding it! Ever! Not one single person!"

"Well ... well ... I've never heard of two children in a floating bathtub rescuing their grandparents from the clutches of one of the most evil pirates in existence, but that doesn't mean it can't happen, does it?" blurted Honk.

Sarah wasn't quite sure how to answer this. When he put it like *that*, the chances of finding a magical wish-granting island almost sounded *more* likely than rescuing their grandparents.

"I suppose you have a point," Sarah quietly admitted. "We shouldn't really rule out *anything* that might increase our chances of saving our grandma and grandpa."

"Exactly!" agreed Honk.

"But this doesn't mean we abandon our rescue mission!" Sarah quickly added. "Searching for the island is strictly a last resort!"

"Of course!"

"Unless . . . do *you* have any idea where this island is supposed to be?" Sarah asked Honk.

"Nobody knows where it is," Honk admitted. "But it's only a matter of time. Someone's bound to find it eventually. It's quite exciting really. The whole search is like an adventure of *epic proportions*, and . . . well, maybe not *epic* proportions, but quite *big* proportions, *large* proportions, maybe. Or *medium to large* at the very least. And there's a bet on who'll find the island first. My money's on Captain Doom. He's so desperate to have his wish granted that he's spent ten whole years searching for it."

"Whoa!" said Charlie. "He must have a *really* important wish."

"Aha! Well! It's funny you should say that, because I happen to know *exactly* what his wish will. . ."

"Did you say his boat was pink?" Sarah quickly interrupted, her eyes locked on to something over Honk's shoulder.

"What? Oh. Yes, pink. But what he wants to wish for is—"

"What kind of boat?" Sarah interrupted again.

"What *kind* of boat?" Honk replied shortly, not too pleased about being interrupted for a second time. "It's an ugly, mutilated monstrosity that looks like all the junk in the seas nailed into one gigantic, churning, crunching, unstoppable deliverer of death that destroys anything that gets in its way. But that's not important right now. What *is* important is that I alone know the secret of Captain Doom's wish, and that secret is—"

"And it's *definitely* pink?" Sarah interrupted again.

"Yes!" Honk bellowed. "It's Pink! Bright pink! That's why they call it the *Bright Pink Ship of Doom*! Now will you please stop interrupting?"

"Yes," said Sarah. "Sorry. It's just, I thought you might like to know that it's right behind us."

CAPTAIN DOOM

Steam, smoke and flames billowed out from various chimneys that protruded from the humongous mass of nails and wood that was the *Bright Pink Ship of Doom*. It looked as if it had been constructed from fifty different ships that had all been smashed up and thrown back together in dozens of different, mismatched pieces. And that's because it *was*. You see, because Captain Doom had never ever stopped the *Bright Pink Ship of Doom*, this meant that the crew had never stopped to make repairs, which meant that any damage to the ship had to be fixed whilst the ship was still moving, which resulted in the *Bright Pink Ship of Doom* looking like a big, pink, sailing junk heap. Massive chunks of other boats had been nailed to the ship to repair holes, branches had been used to splint snapped masts, and old clothes had been used to patch up damaged sails. But, despite its horrific exterior, the deck of the *Bright Pink Ship of Doom* had a calm and relaxed atmosphere, and the only person on board who didn't seem happy to be there was the captain.

As usual, Captain Doom stood behind the tiller, with a telescope pressed to his eye. He was *always* on the lookout for the Island of Unbelievably Cute and Fluffy Bunnies. As were most of his crew, especially the one named Mr Lookout, who was perched way up in the crow's nest amongst those chimneys, munching happily away on his seagull-and-relish sandwich.

Just like all the crewmates on the *Bright Pink Ship of Doom*, Mr Lookout was *not* a pirate. This was because Captain Doom *hated* pirates. Captain Doom was a "scavenger", and according to him, the difference between a scavenger and a pirate is the same as the difference between someone who hunts to survive and someone who hunts for fun – one will take only what they *need*; the other will take whatever they *want*. And according to Captain Doom, that is "uncivilized, disrespectful and downright rude!" And because Captain Doom hated pirates so much, he always made sure to only ever hire the most honest, hard-working, trustworthy *non*-pirates he could find. You may be thinking that this doesn't sound like a very dangerous crew for the Number One Most Dangerous Pirate on the Seven Seas Who Isn't Officially a Pirate, and you would be right. But it was his determination to stop at nothing that made Captain Doom so dangerous. He would literally not stop for *anything*, so if another boat was stupid enough to get in his way, the *Bright Pink Ship of Doom* would plough straight through it, and every last scrap of the wreckage would then be recycled. The rest of what made him so famously dangerous was mostly just gossip and rumours, like "He eats everyone he captures!" and "If you look him in the eyes you will be turned into a pillar of earwax!" and "His crew is made up of vampires and dentists!" but none of these were true. Captain Doom may have been a bit of a grump, but the only malice he harboured was towards pirates. And his crew were not scary at all; they were primary school teachers, nurses, sweet-shop assistants and librarians, who were *mostly* kind happy, polite individuals whom Captain Doom had trained to become top class sailors. I say they were "mostly" kind, happy, and polite because the cannon-loaders were known to get a bit argumentative from time to time, which is quite understandable, considering how difficult their jobs could be.

Mr Lookout's job wasn't too difficult, though;

all he had to do was to look out for two things, and two things only:

1. The Island of Unbelievably Cute and Fluffy Bunnies.
2. Any other ship that got in the way.

And it was at this exact moment, whilst finishing off his seagull-and-relish sandwich, that somehow, through the cloud of smoke that engulfed him, Mr Lookout managed to spot one of these things.

"Ship ahoy!" he bellowed.

"Pirates or non-pirates?" Captain Doom called up to him.

"Looks like pirates, sir!"

If it had been a non-pirate ship, then Captain Doom may have steered around them since they already had all the supplies they could carry for now, but this was not a non-pirate ship. And Captain Doom *hated* not-non-pirate ships. Letting them go was not an option. Captain Doom promptly lowered his telescope, tugged at the large collar of his overcoat, and spun around to face his crew, ready for business. "You know what to do, First Mate Scary Face!" he growled in his deep, rumbling voice as he rubbed his hands in relish.

"Load the cannons?" asked First Mate Scary Face.

"No, bring me a napkin! I just got relish all over my hands!"

First Mate Scary Face quickly passed Captain Doom a towel, then sheepishly retreated.

"Thank you," muttered Doom. "That was disgusting. If I find out who spilled that, they'll be in for a jolly good telling off! Right, well, *now* you know what to do, First Mate Scary Face."

"Load the cannons?" whispered First Mate Scary Face, afraid of getting it wrong again.

"Yes, Scary Face, load the cannons. What do you think? Good grief!"

"LOAD THE CANNONS!" roared First Mate Scary Face.

"LOAD THE CANNONS!" yelled Small and Insignificant Pirate.

"LOAD THE CANNONS!" bellowed Cannon-Loader Number One.

"It's *your* turn to load the cannons," grumbled Cannon-Loader Number Two.

"No, I think you'll find it's yours," replied Cannon-Loader Number One.

"Come on, don't be silly, you know the captain hates it when we argue. Just load the cannons, there's a good man."

"Don't you '*good man*' me! I'll give you to the count of three to load that cannon or I'll make you sorry!" warned Cannon-Loader Number One.

"No, mate, *you've* got to the count of three, or I'll make *you* sorry!" Cannon-Loader Number Two argued.

"One!" they both said.

"Two!" they both said.

"Three!" they both said...

And then one of them did something that made the other one sorry.

ATTACK OF
THE GRANDPARENTS

The *Bright Pink Ship of Doom* was bearing down on the *Bathtub of Certain Death* at an incredible rate, which was not good news for its passengers, but that wasn't all – there was a *third* boat out on those waters, a third boat that was hurtling across the ocean with astonishing speed. A third boat that Sarah, Charlie and Honk had failed to spot. A third boat that they had been certain was heading *away* from them, but somehow, along with the *Bright Pink Ship of Doom*, was now ploughing directly towards them. A third boat that was named the *Vladiator* – the very same boat that Sarah and Charlie were searching for. The very same boat on which Harold and Ethel were being held prisoner.

And on that boat:

CRACK!

Harold and Ethel threw all their weight at the door at the top of the stairs. The door began to splinter, and Vlad began running around in circles, clutching his map for dear life and screaming, "Don't help me! I'm loving this!"

But there wasn't even anyone there to refuse him help. It seemed that even First Mate Ned, Vlad's most loyal companion, had done a runner, and left him to fend for himself.

I told them I didn't do it! I apologized for their loss! Why do they still want to kill me?! Vlad asked himself, hysterically. *The nicer I try to be, the more everyone seems to hate me!*

Vlad had never felt more alone. But suddenly, to his great relief, someone came rushing into the room – First Mate Ned had returned with a hammer and nails, and an armful of wood, and instantly began boarding up the door that Harold and Ethel were now smashing to pieces.

Vlad almost cried with gratitude. Ned had proven himself to be so loyal, so understanding and protective, that for a fleeting instant, Vlad almost felt like someone *did* understand him!

"Yes!" he cheered! "Ned, you're a genius! Keep going! Keep them down there! Keep them away from me!"

Except, yes, you guessed it, he didn't say it *exactly* like that. It actually came out a bit more like this:

"No! Ned, you're an idiot! Stop! Let them out! Bring them to me!"

So Ned, who had been so certain that he was finally doing something that would make Vlad proud of him, stopped boarding up the doors and, with much disappointment and trepidation, began pulling the nails out and taking them back off.

Vlad was aghast. What was Ned doing?! He was

disobeying a direct order! He was putting Vlad's life at risk! And more importantly, Ned, just like everyone else, was *misunderstanding* Vlad. Vlad's heart sank and his panic rose as he watched Ned remove the last of the boards.

Ned turned the lock.

"No, Ned! Stop!" Vlad cried, but what came out was: "Yes, Ned! Keep going!"

Ned opened the door.

"This is so good!" Vlad wailed. "I love it!"

And then Ned ran.

THE SECRET
SEA POLICE

The Secret Sea Police were hard at work on the deck of the SSP *Destroyer* as they raced towards the source of the two emergency calls they had received. The ship moved with such sleek and silent speed that it was almost impossible to hear. And, even better than that, it was almost impossible to *see*. This was because the SSP *Destroyer* was the finest example of seafaring camouflage anybody had ever seen. Actually, to be more accurate, it was the finest example of seafaring camouflage anybody had *never* seen. It was so well camouflaged that is was practically invisible. You could sail straight past it and never know it was there. It was a product of pure genius. A work of art. And you had to not see it to believe it. Its body was painted to look like the sea, and its sails were painted to look like the sky, which made this ship *almost* impossible to see.

I say it was only *almost* impossible to see because there was one little detail that made it stand out slightly – the boat's name was written down the side of the ship in giant red letters:

THE SECRET SEA POLICE DESTROYER!

(The crew had to express their self-pride *somehow!*)

And as if that wasn't impressive enough, each and every officer on board was also painted to look like the sea (except for the lookout, high up in the looky-outy crow's nest, who was disguised as a fluffy little cloud).

The commander of the Secret Sea Police, Tenacious Hunt, was a hero not just to Charlie, but all across the entire north of the seven seas. He was one of the two most dedicated pirate-catchers the world had ever seen. The other most dedicated pirate-catcher the world had ever seen was a man named Voracious Hunt, Tenacious's brother (who also happened to be his enemy). Voracious Hunt was the SSP commander for the *south* portion of the seven seas, and the two brothers were in competition to win the award for The Most Pirate Captains Captured in One Year. Today was the last day of the competition, and the scores could not have been any closer:

Voracious Hunt (South) –
554 Pirate Captain Captures
Tenacious Hunt (North) –
552 Pirate Captain Captures

Tenacious Hunt was just three captures away from beating his brother, and he only had until the end of the day to do it. But capturing pirate captains is a bit like finding your favourites in a box of chocolates – the more of them you take, the harder they are to find – which meant that not only was Tenacious Hunt running out of *time*, he was also running out of *pirates to capture.* So it was all hands on deck on board the SSP *Destroyer* as Tenacious Hunt prepared his officers for the most important captures of his life.

"'Thank you! Thank you!" Commander Tenacious Hunt called as his officers and crew greeted him with rapturous applause on the deck of the ship. "And welcome to another game of ... Catch That Pirate! Ladies and gentlemen, boys and girls, I guarantee you a fun-packed day of pirate-killing adventure. After all, why are we out at sea...?"

Tenacious Hunt cupped a hand around his ear and waited for his audience to shout their well-practised response.

"To catch ourselves some stinking thieves!" the crowd replied as one voice.

"And round one of Catch That Pirate is, as always, a little contest we like to call..."

"Find the Flag!" The crowd cheered and clapped in excitement.

"As you know, a red flag means..."

"MY MATES!" the crowd replied.

"And a black flag means..."

"PI-RATES!!!" The crowd roared, and spat, and shook their fists in hatred.

"So if the flag's not red..."

"We make 'em dead!" the crowd responded, followed by another huge cheer.

Tenacious Hunt raised his hands, gesturing for quiet, and when the quiet came he let it linger. Everyone waited in silence, twitching with eager excitement to hear the words that they cherished so much. And then, after the dramatically long pause, those words finally came:

"LET THE HUNT BEGIN!"

So the hunt began. Every single person on board ran to the sides of the ship, raised their telescopes to their eyes, and searched for the black flags of pirate ships.

"Remember, I need three pirate captains by the end of the day!" Tenacious Hunt added. "Make me proud, people!"

And proud he was, because within seconds he heard an excited cry:

"I've found one!"

Tenacious Hunt was overjoyed. And then...

"I've found one too!" someone else yelled.

Tenacious Hunt was ecstatic! And *then*...

"Another one! I've found another one!" someone else screamed with glee.

Tenacious Hunt almost peed himself with excitement! He could hardly believe his luck! All he had to do now was sink those three pirate ships and he would win that award! It was fantastic news!

Except it wasn't. It was very, very *bad* news, because those three pirate ships that he was about to sink were, of course, the *Bright Pink Ship of Doom*, the *Vladiator*, and the *Bathtub of Certain Death*.

And none of them saw him coming.

MEANWHILE, IN THE BATHTUB...

The SSP *Destroyer* was so well camouflaged that you would need the sight of a bird in order to spot it. And it just so happened that, perched on the side of the *Bathtub of Certain Death*, looking straight out towards the SSP *Destroyer,* was one particularly handsome, green, parrot-y ex-wizard, narrator of this story, who *did* have the sight of a bird – me.

I took to the clouds to get a bird's-eye view of the whole scene, and what I saw was not good – the *Vladiator* was speeding in from the east, the *Bright*

Pink Ship of Doom was ploughing in from the west, the SSP *Destroyer* was sneaking up from the south, and smack in the centre of them all was the tiny little *Bathtub of Certain Death*. And as usual, whilst trapped in my useless green parrot-y form, there was absolutely nothing I could do to help.

"What are we going to do?" shrieked Sarah. "There are two huge boats coming from both sides!" (She hadn't noticed the practically invisible SSP *Destroyer* because, well, it was practically invisible.) "We're going to get crushed!"

And then somehow things managed to get even worse, for, believe it or not, there was something *else* heading towards them – something moving fastest of all, something up in the sky, something that filled the air with a strange noise...

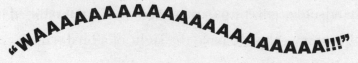

"WAAAAAAAAAAAAAAAAAAAAAAAAA!!!"

MEANWHILE, ON THE SSP *DESTROYER*

Commander Hunt and the rest of the Secret Sea Police were giggling with excitement as their ship quietly crept up alongside the first of the three pirate ships they had spotted – the tiny little bathtub.

"Wait till you see the looks on their faces!" Tenacious Hunt whispered, like a giddy schoolchild about to play the world's best prank as he prepared to give the instruction for his men to drop a barrel full of lead off the end of the plank and straight on to the heads of Sarah, Charlie and Honk.

"They won't know what hit them!" he giggled with feverish excitement.

If the barrel of lead didn't crush them all in an instant, then it would at least sink their bathtub, plunging them into the shark-infested waters.

But just as they were about to drop the barrel, the barrel-pushers became momentarily distracted by a strange noise that filled the sky.

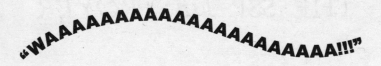

"WAAAAAAAAAAAAAAAAAAAAAAAA!!!"

MEANWHILE, OVER ON THE *VLADIATOR*...

Meanwhile, over on the *Vladiator*, Ethel and Harold were in hot pursuit of Vlad, who, by his twenty-seventh lap of the ship's deck, appeared to be finally running out of energy. His legs were tiring, his strength was waning, and Harold and Ethel were not slowing down!

"Don't help me!" Vlad pleaded with his crew, who were all standing on the deck, watching this rather bizarre chase take place. "*Please* don't help me!"

The crew really felt that they *should* help their

captain, but they knew never to do anything as stupid as to disobey a direct order from Vladimir Death Pirate, so instead they just stood there, gawping, goggle-eyed and slack-jawed as an extremely hairy pair of grandparents chased their captain around his own ship.

"I'm begging you! Please! Just carry on as you are!" Vlad whimpered to his crew as he dragged his exhausted body past them. "I'm really enjoying this! I'm ordering you to all ignore me and leave me to be eaten alive!"

Vlad knew he had no chance against Harold and Ethel; they were like some kind of super-beings – they had teeth that could eat through wood, hair that could grow at the speed of light, and an unstoppable source of energy. The horrible reality of the situation was beginning to dawn on him – they were going to eat him alive.

As I circled overhead, looking down on the tragic misunderstanding playing out beneath me, I could have sworn I heard Vlad's heart begin to break as he realized that he would never get to experience the warm and cosy feeling of being loved and understood by his dad.

I couldn't let this happen.

I couldn't let Vlad suffer like this.

I couldn't let Harold and Ethel face the guilt of biting the fingers, toes, head and bottom off an innocent man. So, for the second time that day, I focused all my energy on returning myself back to a regular genius wizardy human.

I perched on a mast.

I closed my eyes.

I raised my right wing in the air.

And as I turned in a circle, I *forced* that all-important word to the front of my mind – *"UNDO!"*

POP!

I instantly opened my eyes.

Gold sparks rained down around me.

Magic had happened once again!

Then I looked down and, to my astonishment, I saw...

Vlad trip over and fall flat on his face.

The only thing I had managed to undo was Vlad's shoelaces.

Harold and Ethel were on him in an instant. Mouths open wide, teeth bared… But before they managed to eat his head, fingers, toes or bottom, something distracted them from way above, something that emitted a strange sound that filled the sky…

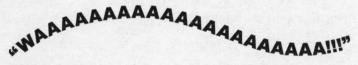

"WAAAAAAAAAAAAAAAAAAAAAAAAA!!!"

MEANWHILE, UP IN THE AIR, SOMEWHERE...

"WAAAAAAAAAAAAAAAAAAAAAA!!!" screamed Cannon-Loader Number Two as he whistled through the air like a human cannonball that had recently been shot from the barrel of Massively Oversized Cannon Number Seven, directly towards a pirate ship.

"I'M SORRRRRRYYYYYYYY!!!!!!!!" he bellowed.

Meanwhile, on the *Bright Pink Ship of Doom*, Cannon-Loader Number One took a pause from loading the cannons, looked up at the wailing dot in the sky, then grunted, "Good."

CANNON
NUMBER TWO

First Mate Ned, who hadn't spotted the tiny little bathtub, or the practically invisible SSP *Destroyer*, watched in horror as a monstrous pink ship churned through the sea towards them, and a strange-shaped cannonball shot away from it, directly towards the *Vladiator*.

"Vladimir Death Pirate, sir?" Ned called nervously. "We're under attack! Someone's firing human-shaped cannonballs at us! What should I do?"

"Wooeeerghhhhh!" was the only noise Vlad could make as Ethel drew her gaze away from the human cannonball and resumed her attempts to chew his face off.

"What should I do, sir?" Ned repeated anxiously.

"Waaaaaaaarghhhhh!!!" Vlad wailed as Harold nibbled dangerously close to his left buttock.

"Sir? Please! We need to do something!" Ned pleaded in terror.

But it was no use. Vlad was so busy moving his body parts out of the way of the gnashing teeth that he didn't really seem to care about man-shaped cannonballs at all. So Ned decided to take matters into his own hands and give the orders himself. He was first mate, after all.

He stepped up on to the toppy end of the ship. He took a deep breath. And then he gave the crew their orders...

"Cannons, please," he whispered.

Oh dear. It had happened again, just like last year, when Vlad had left Ned in charge, and the

153

Vladiator had come under attack from three blind monks in a fishing boat – he had become so terrified that he lost the ability to speak!

"Cannons ... p ... p ... please," Ned whispered again.

Nobody heard a thing.

So he tried it again.

"Plannons geese!" he said, this time managing to raise his voice to a normal talking volume, but unfortunately not making the slightest bit of sense.

Unsurprisingly, the crew were still not paying him a blind bit of notice, so, determined to overcome his fear, Ned punched himself in the arm and told himself to "stop being a nitwit!" He stepped forward, filled his lungs, and much to his own surprise, he emitted an almighty, ear-splitting roar.

"AARRRRRRRRRR!"

The crew stopped. They turned. They gaped.

"AARRRRRRRRRR!" Ned bellowed again,

and this time he pointed at the *Bright Pink Ship of Doom*.

The shipmates all looked at one another, then shrugged in bafflement.

"AARRRRRRRRRR!" Ned roared again, pointing exasperatedly at the huge cannon behind him, then miming a flying cannonball with his hands, then once again pointing to the *Bright Pink Ship of Doom*.

"Ohhhhhhhhhh! I know what he means!" said Freakishly Tall Pirate Who Hops Too Much, who was by far the cleverest pirate on board. "Do as I say, everyone!"

Unfortunately, despite Freakishly Tall Pirate Who Hops Too Much being the cleverest pirate on board the *Vladiator*, he was still actually really rather stupid (it's just that everyone else on board was even stupider), and when Ned had pointed towards the *cannon*, Freakishly Tall Pirate Who Hops Too Much thought that he was pointing to the *toilet*, which was directly *next to* the cannon.

So, Freakishly Tall Pirate Who Hops Too Much gave the order, then BOOOOOOOOM!

They fired the toilet out to sea.

IT FELL
FROM THE SKY

OK, so, let me try to remember this correctly –
we've got the *Bright Pink Ship of Doom* bearing
down at an incredible rate, the *Vladiator* closing
in with astonishing speed, the Secret Sea Police
sneaking up from behind, Cannon-Loader Number
Two shuttling through the sky like a human-
shaped cannonball, and a toilet rocketing through
the clouds like a . . . kind of . . . toilet. And if any one
of these threats reached the bathtub it would mean
certain death for Sarah, Charlie and Honk.

"What *is* that?" Sarah asked, staring up at the WAAAAAAAAAA-ing object that was flying in from the east.

"It looks like – a *man*!" Honk gasped.

"Really?" said Charlie, who hadn't even noticed the mannonball, and was staring up at the toilet that was hurtling towards them from the west. "Looks more like a stinking great toilet to me."

As the steaming, poo-filled bucket came plummeting towards them, Charlie got a better look at it, and his fears were confirmed – it definitely was a stinking great toilet.

"Guys..." he said, trying to warn Sarah and Honk.

But neither of them paid him any attention. Honk reached for Sarah's great big spiky branch, but Sarah snatched it away from his grasp.

"What are you doing?" she demanded.

"I'm trying to protect you!" Honk replied frantically. "There's a flying man hurtling through the sky! Please, give me the branch!"

"No, I need to protect *you two*!" Sarah argued. "It's what I've been preparing for my entire life!"

"Guys!" Charlie repeated. "Toilet!"

"You should have gone before we left!" Sarah barked.

"Here he comes! I can't let anything happen to you!" said Honk, reaching for Sarah's branch and managing to grab the end of it. But Sarah still didn't let go.

"*I* will protect us, Honk!" Sarah yelled.

"AAAARGHHH! SORRY. No, *I* will!"

"Guys!" Charlie called again, now furiously paddling the water with his hands. "It's coming!"

"Well, hold it in!" Sarah ordered as Honk tugged at the very spiky branch.

"Please let go!" Honk begged. "I have to do this! I feel like it's my duty to watch over you both!"

"YOU TWO!" Charlie roared at the top of his voice. "IT'S ALMOST HERE!"

"OK! Fine!" Sarah screamed, finally relinquishing the branch. "Take it, Honk!"

"AAAARGHHH!" screamed Honk, accidentally letting go of the branch as he flinched at the sound of his name.

The big spiky branch spun upwards, high into the air, smashing straight into the bucket of poo and sending it rocketing back home to the *Vladiator*.

But the flying man was still hurtling towards them, and now they had no branch to defend themselves with.

AND THIS FELL
FROM THE SKY TOO

Sarah and Honk's battle for the big, spiky branch had been a complete waste of time because, way up in the sky, Cannon-Loader Number Two overshot the bathtub by a long way.

"WAAAAAAAAAAA!" he continued to wail as he covered his eyes, dropped through a thin, wispy cloud, ripped through a pirate flag, tore through the mainsail, and then...

BOOOOOOOOOOOM!

He smashed into the *Vladiator*, punching a man-sized hole into the deck. But he didn't stop there...

BOOOOOOOOOOOM!

He crashed through the hull of the ship, and ...

SPLOOOOOOOOSH!

... straight into the ocean.

Everyone on board stopped what they were doing and stared with disbelief at the great big hole in the middle of the ship. They listened, mouths agape, to the splashes and grunts of Cannon-Loader Number Two as he clambered back in through the hole in the hull, sloshed his way up the stairs, burst through a doorway, and appeared in front of them, dripping wet and spitting splinters.

"I am *SO* sorry," he panted, shaking his head in embarrassment as he addressed the crew. "I just crashed into your boat!" he continued, still gasping for breath. "Did a little bit of damage to the bodywork. Looks worse than it is, though. If you've got a hammer and nails, I'll get it shipshape for you in no time!"

"My ... my boat is sinking, isn't it?" Vlad stuttered in shock, still being held down by Harold and Ethel. (He had actually tried to say "My boat *isn't* sinking, is it?" but some questions work whether they're said wrongly or not.)

"No, no!" insisted Cannon-Loader Number Two. "It's taking on water, and it is going in a ... downward direction, but I wouldn't say it was *sinking*."

Vlad was so preoccupied by the prospect of his ship sinking that he had completely forgotten about Ethel and Harold. He didn't even notice when Ethel reached for a chunk of the shattered deck.

She held the thick hunk of wood high in the air.

She clenched her eyes shut.

Then, with all her strength, she slammed it down towards Vlad's head.

SPLAT!

MESSY HEADS

The chunk of wood came slamming down towards
Vlad's head, but stopped just an elephant's hair
from impact. Something had caused Ethel to
freeze – something that had come flying out of a
bucket that had soared up and over the side of the
ship. Something that smelled a lot like poo, *looked*
a lot like poo, and, as it splatted straight into her
hair-strewn face, she found *tasted* a lot like poo, too.

"POOOOO!" Ethel shrieked in horror.

She dropped the chunk of wood to the floor

and stumbled backwards, closely followed by a concerned Harold.

"Darling, let me help you! You have a little bit of brown stuff on your..."

SPLAT! The bucket hit the deck, releasing the remaining dollops of sludge into the air, straight into Harold's face.

"POOOOOO!" wailed Harold as he and Ethel frantically crawled away in blind, frenzied circles, spitting and spluttering, tripping over their ridiculously long hair and desperately trying to wipe the poo from their poo-covered faces.

"No!" Vlad cheered as, finally, events seemed to be turning in his favour. He seized his opportunity in a heartbeat, pounced on top of his attackers, tied their hands behind their backs, and, more importantly, tied their powerfully dangerous mouths firmly shut.

Harold and Ethel growled in anger, thinking about what they would do to Vlad if they ever got out of this situation (which they would. Harold and

Ethel were tough cookies. They had been through far worse things than mere splats of face-poo!).

Feeling thoroughly proud of his little victory, Vlad got to his feet and breathed a sigh of relief. He brushed himself off and awaited the huge cheer and round of applause from his crew.

But the cheers didn't come.

Any second now, he thought.

But the cheers still did not come.

Any … second … nnnnnnnow…

Vlad turned around to face his crew, and instantly realized why they weren't cheering – each and every one of them was being held at knifepoint by the entire crew of the *Bright Pink Ship of Doom*.

"Pleasure to make your acquaintance," growled Captain Doom, tugging at the large collar of his overcoat as he turned to face Vlad. "I'd like to invite you to join me on *my* ship … IN THE NASTY STINKING DUNGEON-THING, DOWNSTAIRS!!!"

PRISONERS

Vlad and his crew were ushered off the *Vladiator*, across planks, and on to the *Bright Pink Ship of Doom*, which was quite tricky since both ships were still moving and the *Vladiator* was rapidly sinking, but it was a manoeuvre that Captain Doom and his crew had carried out so many times they could have done it with their eyes shut.

Frizzy-Haired Karen, the jailer on board the *Bright Pink Ship of Doom* (who had quite frizzy hair), was sending Vlad's crew down into the dungeon one at a time, making sure to stop each pirate and confiscate any banned items that they might be carrying.

"Sorry," she told one pirate, "no food or drink allowed inside the dungeon."

The pirate reluctantly handed over his boiled turnip and bottle of mango pop, and then Frizzy-Haired Karen allowed him to enter.

"Next!" she called to the queue of prisoners. Then, as Vlad stepped forward, she put out a hand to stop him. "Sorry, no maps allowed."

"Yes!" Vlad protested, clutching his map close to his chest.

The thought of being separated from his last connection to his father brought him out in a cold sweat – the map was his last hope of finding love and understanding!

"No admittance with a map – rule eighty-eight in *The Pirate Jailer's Handbook*, I'm afraid," she said with a shrug, then held out her hand expectantly.

"Excuse me," First Mate Ned whispered politely,

popping his head over Vlad's shoulder and flashing a nervous smile. "Sorry, couldn't help overhearing, but does *no admittance with a map* mean that if he *doesn't* hand over his map then he can't go in, and he's free to leave?"

Frizzy-Haired Karen shuffled nervously on the spot. This question had not come up in *The Pirate Jailer's Handbook*.

"Erm ... I'll have to check with my supervisor," she admitted. Then, to a large man at the back of the boat, she shouted, "Nige! This bloke wants to know, if he don't hand over his map, does he get to go free?"

"What?" Nige yelled back. "I ... err ... I'll ask Dave. DAVE! What happens if a prisoner doesn't hand over his map, does he get to go free?"

"Errrrrrmmmmmm..." Dave yelled back. "I thiiiiink ... what happens is ... I'll check with Gladys. GLADYS!"

And so it went on for a few more minutes, until someone had to ask Captain Doom, who, of course, knew the exact answer, which gradually worked its way back along the chain of pirates.

"Captain Doom says that if he don't hand over the map he gets to be dead," Dave yelled to Nige.

"Captain Doom says that if he doesn't hand over the map, he gets to be dead," Nige called to Frizzy-Haired Karen.

"Captain says if you don't hand it over then you get to be ... Nige! Did you say *dead* or *fed*?"

"Dead!" Nige yelled at the top of his voice. "D-E-A-D! *DEAD!*"

"Sorry about the wait, gentlemen," Frizzy-Haired Karen said with a forced smile as she turned back to her soon-to-be prisoners. "My supervisor says that if you don't hand over the map then you get to be D-E-A-D dead."

Vlad instantly thrust the map into Frizzy-Haired Karen's hands. But he wasn't about to let it go without a fight, and this resulted in Frizzy-Haired Karen having to ask Captain Doom a whole bunch of other questions, like:

"What happens if he hands over the map, but doesn't let go of it?"

And...

"What happens if he lets go of the map but then clamps himself around my leg?"

And...

"What happens if he gets off my leg, but then rolls around on the floor, sobbing like a baby?"

After a long and difficult struggle, Karen managed to force Vlad into the dungeon, but just as she was about to lock the hatch, a spine-chilling voice rent the air like a clap of thunder:

"WAAAIIIIIIT!"

Captain Doom was using the pointy end of his sword to usher two stray prisoners forward – two stray prisoners who had their hands tied behind their backs, hair down to their knees, and thick brown gunk all over their faces. Harold and Ethel were now completely unrecognizable, and they seemed to be desperately trying to communicate something to Captain Doom, but Captain Doom couldn't have cared less.

"Stick 'em down that hole before they stink out my deck!" he barked, giving Harold and Ethel a kick up the backsides as they stumbled down the steps. (Don't worry, Harold and Ethel were tough cookies. They had been through far worse things than a mere kick up the bum!)

So Frizzy-Haired Karen locked Harold and Ethel down in the dungeon too, and Captain Doom turned to watch the mast of the *Vladiator* sink into the ocean.

"Goooooood!" he quietly growled to himself. "Now, back to work!" he bellowed at his crew. "We're close to the island! I can feel it in my bones! Today is the day I will get to make my wish!"

Well, it *could* be the day he would get to make his wish ... just as long as the Secret Sea Police didn't blow them all out of the water first.

FOLLOW THAT BOAT!

Charlie and Sarah watched the bubbles on the surface of the sea where the *Vladiator* had just disappeared.

"You ... you don't think Grandma and Grandpa were still on that ship, do you?" Charlie nervously asked Sarah.

"No," said Sarah, hotly. "We just saw them take everyone across to the pink ship, didn't we?"

"I didn't see Grandma and Grandpa cross over, though," Charlie said, beginning to panic. "What if they were never even on that boat in the first place? What if we've been following the wrong ship this whole time? What if they're on a completely different ship, on their way to the other side of the world?!"

"They *will* be on the pink ship, Charlie!" Sarah assured him impatiently. "*Lots* of people crossed over! We couldn't see *all* their faces! They will have been there somewhere, they *must* have!"

"Well, maybe we should just start looking for the fluffy bunny island place, anyway," said Charlie. "I mean, even if they are on the pink ship, how are we ever going to catch up with it? It's a massive pirate ship, and we're in a *bathtub*!"

"Aha!" exclaimed Honk, excitedly. "Don't give up hope! This isn't just *any* bathtub!"

"Sorry, I forgot, it's a *pirate* bathtub," Charlie said politely.

"Aha! But it's not just *any* pirate bathtub!"

"Yeah, sure, but is it a pirate bathtub that can keep up with a ship that's as big as a castle?" asked

Charlie, pretty certain that the answer would be no.

But Charlie was wrong – the answer wasn't no – the answer was...

KABLOOOM! Honk pulled a lever on the side of the tub, and something loud and fantastic began to happen.

WHAM – WHAM – WHAM – a series of poles shot out of various parts of the bathtub.

FLUP – FLUP – FLUP – a sail unravelled from each pole and instantly billowed in the wind.

"WHOA!" "WHOAH!" "WOO-HA-HAAA!" Sarah, Charlie and Honk whooped with excitement as the bathtub picked up so much speed that it almost lifted into the air as it skimmed across the waves. There were four sails at the front, extra sails on the mast, sails poking out from the sides of the tub, and there were even sails coming out of sails. Honk's silly little bathtub had suddenly become a jaw-dropping sight, and to prove that point...

Sarah's jaw dropped.

There was no way the *Bright Pink Ship of Doom* would get away from them now.

"This thing is *amazing*!" laughed Charlie.

"I know, Christopher!" said Honk, smiling proudly. "I know."

"We missed our chance!" said Lieutenant Snare, one of the officers on board the SSP *Destroyer*, as she watched in disappointment as the bathtub zoomed away at a speed they would never be able to match. "Everything's ruined!"

"On the contrary," said Tenacious Hunt, with a confident smile. "Everything is *perfect*."

"It is?" asked Lieutenant Snare.

"Have you ever heard the phrase, 'Kill two birds with one stone'?"

"Erm ... not really. Does it mean you want me to kill this annoying parrot that keeps following us?" Lieutenant Snare asked, bemusedly.

"No! The pirates!" barked Tenacious Hunt. "They're all going in the same direction now. In a few moments the silly little bathtub pirates will have caught up with the bright pink scary pirates, and then we fire our cannons and destroy them all at the same time! It's perfect! Except ... well, from this far away I won't be able to see the looks on their faces when they realize they're going to die," he added solemnly.

Then, quickly putting on a happy face, Tenacious Hunt turned to his men and raised his hands for silence as he explained the rules.

"Ladies and gentlemen! Boys and girls! The game continues! And the fun keeps getting funner because our pirates are now grouping into one big prize! And what do we get when our eggs are all in one basket?"

Tenacious Hunt cupped a hand around his ear as his crew cheered their response.

"More dead pirates in dead-pirate caskets!"

THE PLAN

Locked in the dungeon thing of the *Bright Pink Ship of Doom*, surrounded by pirate prisoners, and being the only two people tied up, Harold and Ethel felt extremely vulnerable. They hadn't been so close to this many people in a very long time, and Ethel couldn't help worrying that her birthmark might be on display, but with her hands tied behind her back she was powerless to do anything about it. She needn't have worried though; it was so dark down there that the other prisoners could barely even see each other, let alone any birthmarks. Plus, none of the other prisoners were anywhere near her; they were all huddled in the furthest corner from her and Harold, holding their noses and trying desperately not to inhale their horrible poo-aroma.

"I don't like it down here," one of the prisoners muttered fearfully.

"I do," Vlad groaned in opposite agreement. "I feel very lucky to be here."

"He's right," agreed Ned, "at least we're not dead!"

"Good point!" agreed Freakishly Tall Pirate Who Hops Too Much. "I thought Captain Doom destroyed every pirate he ever came across. Why would he let us live?"

"Well," Gigantic Steve chipped in, "either he's not as horrible as they say he is, or he needs to keep us alive for some reason."

The crew began to discuss what possible reason Captain Doom could have for keeping them alive, but Vlad paid little attention – he was too preoccupied by Harold and Ethel. As much as he disliked their aroma, and the fact that they had tried to kill him, Vlad couldn't help but feel a little sorry for them.

Poor little poo-covered old people, he thought. *They're so upset about losing their daughter. It must be horrible for them right now. Especially with all that poo on their heads, and they're not even able to wipe it off because I tied their hands behind their backs. I should at least go and wipe their eyes and mouths clean for them. Erghh, no, yuck! I should order one of my men to wipe their eyes and mouths clear for them. That would be a nice thing to do.*

So, because Vlad was a nice person, that's exactly what he did ... kind of.

"First Mate Ned, please would you be so good as to push more poo into those people's eyes and mouths?" he asked into the vast blackness, his voice swelling with pride at his own selflessness.

The prisoner's discussion came to an abrupt halt,

and they waited in silence for Ned to reply, but he, unseen in the darkness, was glaring angrily in the general direction of Vlad. He really did not want to do any such thing! Not only was it really mean, but he'd also get pooey fingers! So, for the first time ever, First Mate Ned decided *not* to follow a direct order from his captain, and instead came up with a very convincing lie.

"I would love to, sir, but unfortunately ... erm ... my hands are tied ... to a badger," Ned whispered as he quickly hid his perfectly *not* tied, badger-free hands behind his back.

Vlad cursed his bad luck as he realized that, thanks to his bizarre, badger-shackling captors, he was going to have to do the good deed himself. He took a deep breath, said goodbye to the cleanliness on his fingers, and began shuffling towards the royal stinkers.

Of course, Harold and Ethel didn't know Vlad was actually trying to help them (like everyone else, they thought he wanted to push poo into their eyes and mouths), so, as they heard him shuffle towards them, they began to moan in fear of what he was about to do.

All the other prisoners thought that they were about to witness one of history's worst acts of poo-being-pushed-into-eyes-and-mouths, and they too began to groan in disgust.

And, knowing exactly how pooey his fingers were going to get, Vlad *also* began to groan in disgust.

It sounded like the world's worst choir practice.

And then it was done. The poo removal was over. Vlad backed away, frantically wiping his hands on the bars of the dungeon and voicing his disgust with accidentally opposite words such as "Mmmm!" "Yummy!" "Nice!" and "I *like* this!"

By this point everyone's eyes were beginning to grow accustomed to the dark, and as Harold and Ethel braved a peek through their eyelids, they fell silent in confusion. This hadn't turned out as they had expected *in the slightest*! Their eyes and mouths

hadn't had more poo squished into them at all —
they had been *wiped clean!* (Well, clean-*ish*).

As her eyes continued to adjust to the dark, Ethel
watched Vlad desperately try to wipe his pooey
fingers on the floor, almost crying in revulsion,
and whimpering "Lovely poo poo!" over and over
again.

How strange he is, Ethel thought, *looking like he
means one thing, but* saying *the opposite.* Now that
she thought about it, she realized that he seemed
to say the opposite of what he meant rather a lot,
like...

Like when he had cried for his men not *to help him
escape from Harold and me when he actually* seemed
to be desperate *for help...*

Vlad looked up from his finger-wiping, and
noticed Ethel gazing at him with a look on her face
that he couldn't quite put his finger on.

...and when he said *that he wasn't scared of the
Secret Sea Police, but he* looked *terrified, and...*

Vlad suddenly jumped to his feet as it occurred

to him what Ethel's expression might be ... could it be ... *could* it be...?

...and when he said *that he wasn't sorry about what happened to our darling daughter, but his eyes seemed to be so full of sadness!*

Vlad took a step towards Ethel, barely believing it could be true—

Does she ... does she understand me? he wondered to himself.

She certainly *looked* like she understood him. She seemed to be wearing an expression of sadness, kindness, sympathy and empathy, all at once, which made Vlad feel *certain* that she understood him. But he needed to know for sure, and there was one way to find out: Bravely, he forced himself to take another step towards Ethel, and then he said it – something that Ethel had seriously misunderstood last time he said it to her—

"I *did* murder your daughter," he quietly told her.

Vlad thought that he was telling her that he *hadn't* killed her daughter, but remembering how

Ethel had reacted last time he told her this, he took a quick step back, just in case she tried to attack him again.

But Ethel, realizing that he meant the opposite, did not try to attack him. She didn't scream, or cry, or try to eat *any* of his fingers, toes, head or bottom. She simply smiled (well, as best as she *could* smile with her mouth tied shut), and lovingly tilted her head to one side.

Vlad took another step toward Ethel, *dangerously* close – in biting range! But Ethel didn't even flinch. Instead she leaned forward and rested her head on Vlad's arm.

Vlad could barely believe it – this was the first time anyone had understood him since he was a child!

This was what he had been searching for!

Someone understood him!

Someone *actually* understood him!!

Vlad was ready to sing and dance and cry with happiness when, suddenly, the hatch in the ceiling of the dungeon flew open and Captain Doom's furious face glared in.

"I CAN'T FIND IT ANYWHERE!" Doom roared into the dark and silent dungeon. "If any of you scumbags can tell me how to get to one of those wish-granting fluffy bunnies, I'll let you all live. If not ... there are some sharks out here that are getting hungry!"

Vlad didn't know anything about any "wish-granting fluffy bunnies" (mainly because there was no such thing. Doom had the rules all wrong – it was the *meadow* at the centre of the island that granted the wishes, not the *bunnies*) but Vlad *did* know where there was an entire island full of the cutest fluffy bunnies he had ever seen. So, hoping that this would be good enough for Doom, Vlad jumped to his feet, and, in a bid to help his fellow prisoners, told Doom exactly how to get to the island ... sort of.

"I haven't got a *clue* where it is!" he gleefully announced to Captain Doom. "I've never been there in my life!"

A furious rage erupted inside Captain Doom. He scooped one arm into the dungeon, yanked Vlad out through the hatch in one swift jerk, then slammed him on to the deck.

"EXECUTE HIM!" Doom roared to his crew.

This wasn't *quite* the response Vlad had expected.

Behind him the dungeon was a frenzy of noise as everyone inside tried to explain the correct directions to the Island of Unbelievably Cute and Fluffy Bunnies. But, with everyone shouting at once, it was impossible to make out a single word they were saying.

Doom returned to the hatch, to see what the fuss was about, and there, desperately trying to clamber out of the dungeon thing, were Harold and Ethel, still tied up and still looking like monsters from the brown lagoon.

"Execute these two next!" Doom ordered his crew. "They're stinking up my ship!"

Vlad could barely believe his ears. This wasn't how it was supposed to happen! Just moments ago

Vlad had experienced the best moment of his entire life! He had just found someone who *understood him*! Surely there was supposed to be a "happily ever after" or something?! It couldn't end like this! It just *couldn't*!

But it did.

Vlad was dragged to his feet.

He saw the executioner approach.

He saw the glint of a sword...

The shining blade glimmered in the sunlight as it came slicing downwards.

THOINK! – Vlad's head bounced against the deck of the *Bright Pink Ship of Doom*.

And then, just like that, it was all over.

The wooden deck would be stained blood-red for ever more.

THE END
OF VLAD

"You absolute *IDIOT*!" Captain Doom roared at Clumsy Pete. "How many times am I going to have to talk to you about dropping your sword? The prisoner just tripped over it and bonked his head on the deck, and now you've spilled your cranberry juice trying to help him up! That stain is *never* going to scrub out!"

"Sorry, Captain," Clumsy Pete offered meekly. "It was an accident."

"Well, don't let it happen again!" barked Captain

Doom. "Or I might have an accident with my *own* sword, and *your* head! Now, where were we?"

"I was just about to ask the prisoner how he would like to die today, Captain," Brenda the Executioner explained.

"Very good," grunted Captain Doom. "As you were."

"How would you like to die today, sir?" Brenda the Executioner asked Vlad. "Today we can offer you axe, noose or plank."

"Oh, erm ... *all* of them, please," replied Vlad, rubbing his sore head.

"Oh," said Brenda the Executioner, scratching her head in confusion. "That was the exact opposite of what I thought you were going to say. Most people say *none* of them. I don't even know if we can do *all* of them. Let me just check with the boss."

After a moment of careful deliberation with Captain Doom, Brenda returned with an apologetic look on her face.

"Sorry, sir, but Captain Doom says that there isn't enough rope to spare for a noose, and we lost the axe when we were playing Axe-Frisbee last Easter, so it'll have to be the plank if that's OK with you?"

"Yes, that would be absolutely delightful, thank you," Vlad muttered unhappily.

"Thank you for being so understanding," said Brenda the Executioner. "Now if you'd like to follow me, I'll lead you to your death."

"Fantastic," Vlad grunted as a clap of thunder boomed overhead and a pair of heavily armed pirates shoved him towards the plank. He kept glancing over his shoulder, hoping for one last glimpse of Ethel's understanding face, but she was nowhere to be seen. The only friendly face he could find was that of the kind-hearted parrot that had perched on his shoulder, almost as if to comfort him.

The sky was as dark and bleak as Vlad's future, and Vlad's heart was pounding in his chest as ferociously as the shark tails that were thrashing in the waves below. He couldn't believe this was about to happen. It wasn't fair! He *couldn't* die now! He *had* to have a happy ending!

Any minute now something is going to come along to save my life, Vlad reassured himself. *Annnny minute now...*

"Would you mind jumping now, please, sir? Only I've got those two hairy stinkers to execute too," Brenda explained.

Yup, thought Vlad. *Any minute nowwwwww ... someone is definitely going to save me.*

His heart leapt in expectation when he felt someone tap him on the shoulder. But then his heart sank again when he saw that it was merely Brenda the Executioner handing him his map.

"You can have this back now," she said. "It might help you sink quicker."

Then Vlad suddenly realized that nobody was going to save him. He was all on his own.

But the courageous parrot disagreed.

I raised my right wing...

"Right, I'm going to give you to the count of three, and then I want you to jump, OK?" Brenda the Executioner told Vlad. "One..."

Vlad began to panic.

I closed my eyes...

"Two..."

Vlad looked all around for some means of escape, but there was nothing, just water, sharks and more water.

I turned in a circle.

"Three."

Vlad did not jump.

The word "undo" was just beginning to form in my mind when I suddenly became distracted by what Brenda the Executioner said next.

"What am I going to have to do to get you off this plank?" she asked Vlad.

"Well, you could let me back on to the ship, then set me free," Vlad suggested ... except, in opposite speak, it sounded a *little* bit more like this:

"You could start by giving me a good, hard shove!"

So that's exactly what she did.

HARD RAIN

As the bathtub raced towards the *Bright Pink Ship of Doom*, an angry storm rolled in from behind, hammering the bathtub, along with Sarah, Charlie and Honk, with a heavy shower of rain, which quickly turned into a bombardment of hailstones. The waves began to swell into angry peaks, and a distant thunder rumbled across the sky.

This was bad news.

It was bad news because no one had brought their waterproofs. It was bad news because the waves were ten times taller than their tiny little bathtub. But it was *mostly* bad news because the deafening claps of thunder made it impossible to hear the sound of the cannons being fired at them from the SSP *Destroyer*.

A humongous hailstone hit the bathtub with a CLANG like a church bell.

"Would you look at that!" gasped Honk. "That hailstone's the size of an apple!"

As he bent over to pick it up, a cannonball from the SSP *Destroyer* ripped through the air, skimming the back of Honk's head before landing in the ocean with a giant

SPLOOOOOOOOSH!

"And *that* one was the size of a *cannonball!*" Charlie shrieked.

"Not to worry, Charlie, m'lad, *Certain Death* can easily outrun this storm," said Honk, pulling yet another lever and causing the bathtub to pick up even more speed.

Honk was right, the bathtub *could* outrun the storm – but it wasn't able to outrun the cannon fire.

BOOOOOOOOOOOM!

came another thundering crash of the SSP's cannons, and another cannonball rocketed towards the bathtub. Then another. And another. And another...

These ones would not miss.

BROWN ALERT!

The crew of the *Bright Pink Ship of Doom* had no idea they were being chased by the tiny little *Bathtub of Certain Death,* and the crew of *Certain Death,* still mistaking cannon fire for thunder, had no idea they were being chased by a cluster of cannonballs, and the cannonballs … well, they didn't know anything, they were just cannonballs.

"Aren't we going a bit too fast?" Sarah called to Captain Honk as they approached the *Bright Pink Ship of Doom* at an alarmingly high speed.

"What?!" cried Honk, struggling to hear her over the deafening booms of thunder and cannon fire. "You want to go *faster*?! Are you serious? I don't think we *can* go any faster!"

"No!" yelled Sarah, pointing ahead to the huge ship that they were about to sail straight into. "We're *going too fast*!"

"You're going to *fart*?!" Honk bellowed, laughing way too hard.

"NOOO!" Sarah hollered. "GOING! TOO! FAST!"

Honk suddenly stopped laughing.

This was serious news.

He couldn't believe Sarah hadn't told him sooner!

"You're *going* to *poo* in the *bath*?!" he gasped.

He couldn't let this happen! Honk didn't waste a second! He jumped into action, pushed the small brass levers on the side of the tub, and all of the extra sails instantly rolled up and snapped away into their hidden compartments. The bathtub rapidly slowed down. The cannonballs rapidly began to catch up. The bathtub drew level with the *Bright Pink Ship of Doom*, and Sarah, Charlie and Honk each breathed a sigh of relief.

And *then* they noticed the incoming cannonballs.

KABLAM!

A dark and heavy object crashed straight into the bathtub.

It was a direct hit.

EMERGENCY STOP

The dark, heavy, fast-moving object slammed into the bathtub, and Sarah knew that this would finally mean certain death for *Certain Death* – there was no way a bathtub could withstand cannon fire. But when she opened her eyes, she was surprised to see that there was no cannonball-sized hole in the bathtub, *Certain Death* was not filling with water, and best of all, no one was dead! In fact it was quite the opposite – someone else had *arrived*.

Directly above them a pirate had been pushed

to his certain death, but thanks to pure luck (and a dash of coincidence), he had instead fallen straight *into Certain Death.*

Sarah and Charlie stared at this tall stranger, dressed entirely in black, with his bushy black beard, and they knew that they ought to be terrified; yet, strangely, they weren't. There was something about him – not just his face, but ... *him.* He seemed to just ooze kindness, and the twins found that they instantly trusted him.

Vlad whipped his head around, wild with amazement and relief at not being dead.

"This is AWFUL!" he cheered in opposite speak. "This is the worst day of my life! I hate you! I hate you all! I'M NOT ALIVE!"

And that's when Sarah and Charlie both realized that they didn't like him so much after all. Honk, on the other hand, was more bothered by the two dozen cannonballs that were plummeting towards them.

But neither the cannonballs above nor the evil

pirate in their boat were *anything* compared to the threat that was immediately in front of them...

Directly alongside the bathtub, up on the *Bright Pink Ship of Doom*, Brenda the Executioner was preparing to do away with Harold and Ethel when something up ahead suddenly caught her eye...

Something extremely BIG.

Something extremely close.

Something extremely island-shaped.

"Erm, Mr Lookout?" she called to Mr Lookout. "Have you seen..." But she didn't get to finish that question because...

KERRRASHHHHHHH!

The *Bright Pink Ship of Doom* sailed straight into the stony beach of the huge island-shaped thing. It slammed to a sudden and violent halt, and the crew were sent flying through the air.

Then it was the bathtub's turn – Sarah, Charlie, Honk and Vlad all turned in time to see the shore of an island hurtling towards them. The bathtub

slammed into the beach, and Sarah, Charlie, Honk and Vlad were all hurled out, like rag dolls from a sling.

As the humans flew up, the cannonballs fell down, and both boats were turned into Swiss cheese.

It was the luckiest crash any of them could have ever hoped for, not just because it saved them from the cannonballs but because the island they had crashed into was a very special one indeed.

THE RAIN OF
QUEEN ETHEL

"Well, that could have been a lot worse!" Honk said cheerfully as he, Sarah, Charlie and Vlad landed in a big, soft sand dune. "I thought, for a moment there, we were going to get completely and utterly..."

SPLAT!

Harold and Ethel fell from the sky, like giant, poo-covered, king-and-queen-shaped raindrops, landing directly on top of Honk and smooshing him into the ground like a giant insect.

"No!" screamed Sarah and Charlie as they rushed

forward to help Honk. But the smelly, mumbling, hairy, muck-covered creatures got to their feet, blocking Sarah and Charlie's path, and then began stumbling towards them. Sarah and Charlie took one look at these horrific monsters and their "running away" training instantly kicked into action.

"RUN!" Sarah cried, and both she and Charlie fled, as fast as they could, straight towards the centre of the island.

Harold and Ethel could barely believe who they had just seen – Sarah and Charlie were *right there*, on the very same island! But the old king and queen of Angerland were still so covered in hair and poo that even their own grandchildren didn't recognize them! They tried calling after them, but with their mouths tied shut, it just sounded like they were growling and roaring! So, determined not to lose them again, Harold and Ethel shook their poo-tangled hair out of their eyes and did their best to keep up with their grandchildren.

Vlad was in equal disbelief – just when he

thought he had lost the strange, special lady who understood him, he had found her again! So, seeing Ethel running off towards the centre of the island, he sped off after her, too.

Honk, who the others were certain must be dead, suddenly jumped to his feet with a look of pure elation on his face. That knock on the head had done something! For the first time in years he was remembering something about who he really was...

"I REMEMBER!" he howled in delight, throwing his arms up in the air. "My memory is back! I remember my mum, I remember my dad, I remember how I got this dent in my head, and I even remember who I really am! My name isn't *Honk* at all! My name is..."

KATONNNNNNNNNGGGGGGGG!

The bathtub dropped from the sky, completely flattening him into the sand and knocking the memory clear out of him, which wasn't very nice. But it was a whole lot nicer than what was awaiting the others.

THE ISLAND

Captain Doom picked himself up on the stony beach, looked around at the island they had crashed into, and knew in an instant that he had finally found the place he had spent so long searching for. I'm not sure how he was so certain that this was the Island of Unbelievably Cute and Fluffy Bunnies – maybe it was because he had spotted some telltale rabbit burrow holes, or perhaps it was because his allergy to bunny fur was suddenly playing up, or there was a small chance he had seen the huge sign in front of him that read:

"This is it!" he positively screamed with delight as he ran across the beach. "This is it! I've found it! I FOUND IT!!! The Island of Unbelievably Cute and Fluffy Bunnies! THE ISLAND OF UNBELIEVABLY CUTE AND FLUFFY BUNNIES!!!!"

Still thinking that he needed to find a bunny to make his wish come true, Doom raced off in search of one of the fluffy little creatures.

Sarah and Charlie continued to run away from the stinking monsters that were hobbling after them. They ran through dense woodland, dodging trees, ducking branches, and jumping gigantic roots, when suddenly they came upon a clearing. The storm had subsided, and as they stepped into the clearing, Sarah and Charlie found themselves in a beautiful, lush green meadow, bathed in sunlight. And on the other side of the meadow was a huge, towering mountain, where a small waterfall splashed into a stream.

"What is this place?" Charlie whispered in awe.

"It's like a paradise!" Sarah gasped.

"It's a cesspool of filth!" Vlad whispered as he ambled up alongside the twins, overjoyed to be back at the place where he had discovered all of those little rabbits that he adored so much. But his joy slowly evaporated as he struggled to understand why none of those little rabbits were there *now*. Instead of the thousands of bunnies that *had* been there, there were now thousands of tiny, bunny-sized graves. Vlad's knees began to buckle as he came to the only explanation he could think of – some cruel and nasty person had come along and ordered for all the bunnies to be killed! He almost began to weep at the thought of it.

All those adorable little bunnies, he reminisced. *If I ever find out who's responsible for this, I'll ... I'll ... I don't know, but it'll be bad!*

Captain Doom was the next one to appear in the beautiful meadow. His face was, at first, lit up with glee and excitement, but when he noticed the thousands and thousands of unbelievably small, bunny-sized graves, a look of horror washed over him.

"The bunnies?" he said, looking at the others. Then he saw the look of sorrow on Vlad's face. "The bunnies!" he gasped, falling to his knees in despair. "Where are the bunnies?"

But it was horribly obvious where all the bunnies were.

"Why does the Number One Most Dangerous

Pirate on the Seven Seas care so much about the bunnies?" Charlie whispered to Sarah.

"How can I make my wish without any bunnies?" Captain Doom wailed.

"Ohhhh," Sarah whispered back to Charlie, "he thinks the *bunnies* grant the wishes, not the meadow!"

Harold and Ethel were next to emerge from the woods, and despite being desperate to be reunited with their family, they too paused to take in the sombre sight of so many little rabbit graves.

Nobody spoke.

Nobody moved.

They all just stood and stared in hollow silence – a silence that would soon be replaced with screams.

SOMETHING WICKED
THIS WAY COMES

Captain Doom was kneeling in the long grass, his eyes clenched shut as he sobbed for the absent bunnies. The hobbling, long-haired, poo-covered Harold and Ethel creatures were standing beside him and ... well, it looked as though they were *comforting* him. This didn't make sense to anyone. Why would Harold and Ethel try to comfort the same nasty pirate (who wasn't officially a pirate) who had just tried to have them killed? (Unless they weren't comforting him at all. They may have been trying to tickle him with their elbows. It was hard to tell with their hands tied behind their backs.)

"Why, oh why?!" wailed Captain Doom. "How can this be happening? I'll never be able to make my wish now!"

Sarah stepped forward, to try to explain that you didn't actually need *any* bunnies to make a wish, but she stopped when Doom exploded with yet another outburst of sorrow.

"It was all for nothing!" he sobbed. "These last ten years, wasted! Oh, how I wish the bunnies were back, so I could make my wish!" Captain Doom wailed at the top of his voice.

And then, all of a sudden, Captain Doom fell silent.

His eyes widened in surprise.

Then he scrambled to his feet.

"Did you feel that?" he gasped at the stinky brown creatures beside him.

Harold and Ethel looked at one another, then shook their heads – no.

"Did anybody else feel that?" Captain Doom asked the others.

"Feel what?" asked Sarah.

"It moved!" Captain Doom gasped in amazement. "The ground moved! Look!"

Everyone gathered around to watch, and sure enough, the ground beneath Doom's feet suddenly heaved upwards, causing Doom to stumble backwards.

Vlad clutched his map to his chest, squealing in shock as the ground continued to shake and buck.

There, directly in front of them, was a small bunny grave, and it was not behaving in the way that a bunny grave should — it appeared to be *opening*!

The earth rolled, then cracked, then crumbled, and fresh soil began to appear at the opening, almost as if. . .

"Something's trying to get out of it!" Captain Doom exclaimed in excitement.

"And it's not just that one," Sarah said in a tone of dread. "Look!"

They all looked across the meadow to see every

single grave swell and ripple with movement. There was barely half an elephant of ground that *wasn't* moving. It looked almost as if the meadow was a grassy green ocean, undulating with waves. And then from one of those rippling green waves burst a small creature. It was about the size of a cat-sized bunny, with large back feet and prominent teeth.

Another bunny climbed out of the ground. Then another. And another. But there was something strange about these bunnies. They were not cute. They were not fluffy. And there was definitely something ... *wrong* with them.

"I think your wish came true," Sarah said, grimly, to Captain Doom. "The bunnies are back."

"Some of these bunnies don't have any ... eyes," muttered Charlie, as he slowly began to back away.

"Or fur," added Sarah. "Or skin, or flesh, or blood, or..."

"They're skele-bunnies!" Charlie whispered.

"They're *zombunnies*," Sarah whispered back.

More and more of these creatures were clambering out of the ground, and before long, the meadow was swarming with zombunnies.

"I like it," Vlad groaned in fear as he began to run away from them. "I like it a lot!"

His movement seemed to attract the zombunnies' attention.

They watched him run.

They arched their backs.

And then they prepared themselves for attack.

"Run," said Charlie.

"Run?" scoffed Captain Doom.

"Yes," said Sarah, "run!"

"Hmmmm!" agreed Harold and Ethel. "HMMMMM!"

So they ran.

And so did the zombunnies, all of them, straight after the humans.

SOMEONE DIES

"Where are you going?" Captain Doom called after Sarah, Charlie, Vlad, and the royal stinkers. "Don't run away! They just want to play!"

One particular zombunny was heading straight for him, so he crouched down to greet it.

"Come on! Come to Auntie Doom!" he cooed, as if playing with a boisterous puppy. "Who's a cute little schmoopsie-poo? Yes, you are! Yes, you are! Come to Auntie Doom so I can make my wish."

But the closer the zombunny got the less brave Captain Doom became.

"Who's a pretty little ... angry-looking ... growling ... snarling ... AAAAARGHHHHHH!" Captain Doom jumped to his feet and sprinted away as fast as he could. "Run!" he bellowed. "Run away!"

"What are they?" cried Charlie. "Why is this happening?"

"It was *him*," Sarah yelled, pointing at Captain Doom. "He wished for the bunnies to come back, and his wish came true! They came back — *from the grave!*"

"But that can't be right!" cried Captain Doom. "There were no bunnies! And the only way a wish can come true is if there are bunnies!"

Sarah would have liked to explain how Captain Doom had been mistaken, but she, like everyone else, was too out of breath to bother.

The zombunnies seemed to be closing in from every direction now, moving in, tighter and tighter, until Vlad, Charlie, Sarah, Harold, Ethel and Captain Doom found their path blocked by the huge mountain in front of them, and the mass of zombunnies behind them.

There was nowhere left to run.

They were trapped.

Charlie frantically tried to climb the mountain, but it was impossible – it was a sheer sheet of rock, and he soon gave up. The six of them stood with their backs against the rock, and watched as the sea of angry zombunnies edged towards them, their bunny teeth glinting in the sunshine.

"What are we going to do?" whimpered Charlie.

Nobody had an answer, except for Vlad, who, knowing a thing or two about animals, told them that they needed to stay calm, and quiet, and try not to provoke them ... kind of.

"We should scream and shout and make threatening movements," Vlad whispered. "Or maybe taunt them with nasty chants, then throw rocks, and tease them with sticks."

"Hmm hmm hm hmm-hmmmm-hmm!" Harold mumbled desperately.

"I think it's trying to say something," Captain Doom observed.

"He wants his ropes tightening," Vlad informed them.

"Hmm hmm hm hmm-hmmmm-hmm!" Harold repeated frantically.

"It seems like it's quite important. Maybe someone should untie its face," Sarah suggested.

"HMMMM!" Harold agreed, nodding vigorously.

"But it's all ... you know – pooey!" Captain Doom said.

But Vlad was already on it, using a stick to slip the rope off Harold's head, then rapidly hurling the stinking stick over his shoulder and up the mountain, where it hit something with a CLONK! Only the ears of a parrot could have heard the sound of a rather large something beginning to fall from up on the cliff.

"Yum," Vlad complained, covering his nose with his arm. "I love poo."

"Quickly!" Sarah warned. "The zombunnies look like they're about to attack!"

"Squawk!" I panicked, looking up and wondering what big dark something was plummeting towards us.

The rope slid from Harold's face and he took a deep breath of air.

"Come on! What were you trying to tell us?!" demanded Captain Doom.

"I've got an idea!" Harold exclaimed in a voice that was unrecognizably dry and croaky from having his mouth tied shut for so long.

The zombunnies edged closer still – a sea of little skeletons, all growling at once, and looking ready for the kill.

"Squawk!" I repeated, trying to warn the others of the large falling object.

But the others ignored me as they waited anxiously for Harold to continue.

"I think. . ." Harold began.

"Yes?" Sarah impatiently urged the strange, croaky, creature.

"I think. . ." Harold repeated, struggling to catch his breath.

"Slowly, woman!" Vlad barked at Harold.

"I think," said Harold, for a third time. "I think that all of us should. . ."

And then a mountain goat fell from above and landed on poor Harold's head.

And then he died.

THE END

Ooh! No! Hang on...

That's not how it ends!

I can't end a story with one of the characters dying!

What was I thinking?

Sorry.

Keep reading.

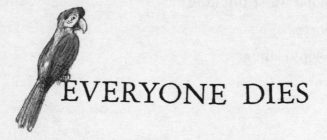# EVERYONE DIES

So, where was I? Oh, yes. Things were looking bad.

We were completely surrounded.

There was no escape.

The zombunnies were about to attack.

And Harold was dead.

I circled overhead, desperately wanting to attempt my "undo" spell for a third time but terrified that I might just make things worse again. The last thing they all needed was for their shoelaces to come undone and for their hair to grow in front of their eyes!

Speaking of which, Vlad was helping the Ethel-shaped, poo-covered, hairy monster in her desperate attempts to resuscitate the Harold-shaped, poo-covered, hairy monster, but they were having zero success. (Harold was a tough cookie though. He'd been through far worse things than mere death!)

"This is the worst day of my life," Sarah groaned, turning away from the sad sight (it would have been even worse if she'd known that the poo-covered dead man with a goat on his head was actually her grandpa). Desperate for some kind of weapon, she searched the ground for something to defend herself with, and finally settled on a large, banana-shaped rock. But as she raised it, menacingly, at the thousands of zombunnies, she slowly realized just how useless it would be.

"I really do not like this." Charlie shuddered, staring out at the thousands of angry zombunnies. "Do you think we're going to die?"

"Yes," said Captain Doom, sadly. "And I'm afraid I shall die without ever getting to make my wish."

"How many times do I have to tell you? You already made your wish!" Sarah growled at him. "These zombunnies – *they're* your wish!"

But Captain Doom either didn't hear this, or he just *chose* not to hear it, because he didn't respond in any way.

"Do you really think we're going to die?" Charlie asked, looking up at Captain Doom with tear-filled eyes.

"Absolutely. No doubt about it," Captain Doom confirmed. "Not only that, but..."

Captain Doom paused when he saw the anguished look on Charlie's face. The sadness and the fear in the boy's eyes gave Captain Doom a peculiar feeling, a feeling that he hadn't experienced in a very long time – it gave him a strange urge to be ... to be *nice!*

"What I mean is..." continued Captain Doom, "we *are* going to die, because *everybody* dies sooner or later, but what I meant to say was ... not today." He clapped an encouraging hand on Charlie's shoulder, almost knocking Charlie sideways.

A small smile cracked the corners of Charlie's mouth. The kindness from Captain Doom had given Charlie a brand-new feeling – *courage*. And without even thinking about what he was doing, Charlie pulled Captain Doom's sword from the scabbard on Captain Doom's belt, then jumped forward, slashed the blade in front of the zombunnies, and cried out:

"My name is Charlie! I'm on a mission to find my grandparents! And now I wish to leave!"

To everyone's amazement, each and every one of the one thousand eight hundred and fifty-two zombunnies took a step backwards.

Feeling more encouraged, Charlie took another lunge forward, slashed with the sword, and said it again.

"My name is Charlie! I'm on a mission to find my grandparents! And now I wish to leave!"

This time the zombunnies took *two* steps back!

Again! Charlie lunged forward, slashed his sword, and bellowed across the meadow:

"My name is Charlie! I'm on a mission to find my grandparents! And now…"

Charlie's bravery suddenly evaporated, and he wondered what on earth he was doing! He was completely surrounded by angry zombunnies, and he wasn't even any good with a sword!

"And now…" he continued, not sounding quite so commanding. "And now … and now it'd be really nice if you could just clear a path and, you know, kind of, let us go … please. If you wouldn't mind. Thank you."

The zombunnies stared at Charlie for an unnervingly long time, and then, slowly, one by one, they began to clear a path.

"Good work, Charlie!" Captain Doom roared with delight.

"Awful!" agreed Vlad. "You're an idiot!"

Then, in a long, narrow line, everyone followed Charlie as he nervously tiptoed his way across the narrow clearing amongst the zombunnies.

"Thank you," Charlie whispered politely,

turning to shuffle sideways so as not to step on any zombunny toes. "I'm not a baby any more!" he whispered to himself. "I did it! I was brave! I was the strong one!"

"It really is jolly kind of you!" Captain Doom said to the zombunnies with uncharacteristic kindness. "Thank you *ever* so much. Excuse me, thank you, thank you, sorry, oops! Mind your toes! Sorry, thank you."

"Not sorry!" Vlad whispered politely to the zombunnies as he edged down the pathway with Harold's limp body over his shoulder. "I hope that hurt! Did it on purpose!"

Eventually, they had all made it through.

Charlie gave a sigh of relief, and said "Whoooh!"

Sarah gave the zombunnies a grateful little smile.

Ethel, whose tears for poor old Harold were soaking into the rope in her mouth, said, "Hmmm hmmm hm hm hmmm hmm hmmm."

And Captain Doom looked out at all the bunnies

that he had spent so long searching for. Then he stepped forward, removed his hat, and said:

"I know that this girl says that I already made my wish, and I know it's a one-wish-only deal, but if it's OK with you, I'd like to try another one, you know, just in case. You see, I've been searching for you bunnies for so many years, and I . . . I just want to ask, please. . . I mean, *I wish* that. . ."

"Hoooweeee!" exclaimed Vlad as he came tramping towards them with Harold slung over his shoulder, panting for breath and babbling in opposite speak. "I'm certainly not glad that that's over. I wish they'd chase us again!"

I'm sure you can guess what happened next:

The zombunnies arched their backs. . .

They lowered their heads. . .

And the chase continued.

ESCAPE FROM ZOMBUNNY ISLAND

The rampaging horde of zombunnies snapped ferociously at their heels as Vlad, Doom and the royals raced through the woods – dodging trees, ducking branches, and jumping roots.

"He's not that bad, is he?" panted Charlie as he struggled to keep up with Sarah.

"What?" gasped Sarah.

"Captain Doom, he's not as bad as they make him out to be. He actually seems kind of. . ."

"Charlie! We're about to be eaten alive! Shut up! And run faster!"

Charlie did shut up, and he did run faster, straight into an upturned bathtub.

"There you are!" cheered Honk, scrambling out from beneath the wreckage of *Certain Death*. "I thought I'd lost you!"

"Honk! You're alive!!!" Charlie roared with delight. **"AAAARGHHH! SORRY,"** screamed Honk, clearly still afraid of his own name.

"We thought you were dead!" Charlie explained.

"Well, no, actually I. . ."

"You'll *both* be dead if you don't shut up and start running!" barked Sarah.

Honk turned to see the horde of vicious, undead bunnies ploughing towards them. He shrieked in terror, and he and Charlie hurriedly joined the others in their manic race from certain death.

They were running as fast as they could, but the zombunnies were still catching up with them. Zombunny teeth nipped at their heels, and Vlad, who was still carrying Harold over his shoulder, had to shake some of them off his legs several times. Sarah knew that if they wanted to stay alive, they were going to have to find safety, and fast.

"I wish they'd stop chasing us! I wish they'd stop chasing us!" Charlie repeated over and over again.

"You only get one wish," Captain Doom told him, sadly, "and you already wished to leave."

"You try it then, Sarah!" Charlie shouted to his sister. "You didn't make a wish!"

"YOU HAVE TO BE IN THE CENTRE OF THE ISLAND!" Sarah roared furiously. "Now stop wasting time with wishes and let's get to the water! There's no way those zombunnies will be able to swim!"

Within minutes they were at the beach. They scrambled over the dunes, scrabbled across the pebble beach, and then threw themselves into the water, splashing out to sea.

Charlie suddenly stopped dead.

"What about the sharks?!" he gasped.

But it wasn't the sharks they needed to worry

about – there was something far more deadly in the water...

Right before their eyes, they saw the water rise up in front of them. It was rising up in columns, human-sized columns, human-*shaped* columns! And then one of the columns opened its eyes.

"Surprisey-monkey!" beamed Tenacious Hunt, grinning from ear to ear.

Charlie recognized him in an instant. He recognized them *all* because those columns of water were not columns of water at all; they were the Secret Sea Police in their camouflage paints. Charlie, still believing the SSP to be valiant and honourable heroes, punched the air and whooped with delight.

"It's the Secret Sea Police! We're saved!"

"Congratulations!" cheered Tenacious Hunt. "You did it! You all got away from those creepy little dead rabbit things! You won! And now, allow me to present you with your prizes. That's right, there are no losers here today. Each and every one of you has won a lifetime's supply of ... CERTAIN DEATH!"

OFF WITH
THEIR HEADS

They never would find out whether the zombunnies could swim or not because, just as those little critters reached the water's edge, each and every one of the zombunnies were blasted back into the sand dunes by a well-aimed bombardment of cannonballs from the SSP *Destroyer.* Vlad, Death, Honk and the royals (including Harold, who was still slung over Vlad's shoulder) were safe. (Well, safe from the bunnies at least.) They had been successfully transported to the SSP *Destroyer*, where they were now in the hands of the murderous Secret Sea Police, and Charlie found himself standing just two elephants from Tenacious Hunt, his all-time hero, so he seized this opportunity to explain the whole misunderstanding to him.

"Excuse me, Mr Hunt," Charlie began, politely.

Tenacious Hunt turned to see who was talking to him, then, noticing who it was, he crouched down to Charlie's level and smiled at him, warmly.

"What can I do for you, champ?" he asked, gently.

"There's been a mistake, you see. I'm not a pirate. And these people – well, they're actually nice people," Charlie explained.

"They are?" said Hunt, looking concerned. "But they *are* pirates, aren't they?"

"Well, some of them are, but..."

"They were sailing in pirate ships, weren't they?" Hunt interrupted gently.

"Well, yes, but..."

"Well, in that case they must all be horrible pirates!" Hunt said, giving Charlie a reassuring smile. "Only pirates would sail on pirate ships, and there's no such thing as a *good* pirate!"

"But that's the thing, you see. . ."

"Pirates are the *bad guys*," whispered Hunt, gently placing a hand on Charlie's shoulder. "They steal, and they cheat, and they lie, and that's why you're lying to me right now, isn't it – because *you're* a pirate?"

"No! I. . ."

"You're a tiny, cute little boy-sized pirate captain, and you're trying to trick me, because that's what pirates do. You and your pirate captain sister, and the rest of your pirate captain family here."

"No, we're not. . ."

"Enough!" barked Tenacious Hunt, rising to his full height and turning his back on Charlie to address his crew. "I've caught enough pirate captains to ensure my brother will never defeat me! Not only will I win that award, but I'll probably hold the world record for hundreds of years to come! And now the pirate scum must die ... *all* of them!"

"But ... but, sir..." stuttered Lieutenant Snare, "I don't think they're *all* pirate captains, I mean, some of them are just children..."

"Don't argue, Lieutenant Snare!" Hunt bellowed. "They're pirates if I say they're pirates! I've got an award to win, in case you've forgotten! Now send them to the head-chopper-offer!"

The prisoners were marched to the centre of the ship and shoved to their knees in front of the head-chopper-offer.

The head-chopper-offer was a horrendous yet simple contraption that consisted of a long row of holes in the side of the boat through which the prisoners would poke their heads, and a verrrrrrry long blade that would drop down and pop their heads off, straight into the ocean.

"May I introduce our brand-new head-chopper-offer!" announced Commander Hunt, all smiles and teeth for the benefit of his audience. "I would explain what it does, but everything you need to know is in its name. Any questions? No? Good. Come along now, chop-chop, and we can have this all over and done with in time for dinner. Not *your* dinner of course, pirate *scum*. You'll all be dead. But *we'll* still be having dinner. Something nice, hopefully. Shepherd's pie, I think it is today. Can't wait!"

"He doesn't seem as heroic as I imagined him to be," Charlie muttered to Sarah as his head was shoved through one of the many head holes of the head-chopper-offer.

"He doesn't really, does he?" Sarah quietly agreed.

"In fact, he actually seems kind of like ... a *bad guy*," Charlie observed, unable to keep the disappointment from his voice.

"He does really, doesn't he?" Sarah agreed again.

"Everybody comfortable?" bellowed Commander Hunt. "Good! Now, I'll count down from three, and what I want you all to do is go —

'AAAAAAAARGHHHHHH!!!!!' Then I'll pull this lever, the blade will go *CHOP*, and your heads will go...?"

"PLOP!" cheered his crew.

"That's right," continued Hunt, rubbing his hands with eager excitement. "There's really nothing to it. I'll be doing all the hard work. All you need to do is kneel there and enjoy the view. OK? Heeeeere we go!"

"Wait," Captain Doom said to Sarah. "Before, did you say that you *don't* need a bunny to make a wish, you just need the centre of the island?"

"Yessss!" Sarah said through gritted teeth. "When will this ever sink in?!"

"*All* of the centre, or just *some* of it?" asked Doom.

"What do you mean — *just some of it?* How can you have just some of it?"

"Remember what you have in your hand," said Doom.

Sarah raised her left hand. Her eyes widened and her mouth dropped open as she began to realize what Captain Doom was getting at – there, clutched tightly in her fist, was the banana-shaped rock she had picked up from the centre of the island.

"You brought the centre of the island back with you!" Charlie whispered in amazement. "And you never even made your wish!"

"Do you think it'll work?" asked Doom.

"It's worth a try!" said Charlie.

"Hmmm hmmm!" agreed Ethel.

"Wouldn't bother if I were you," Vlad said encouragingly.

"Wait," said Honk. "*That* was the Island of Unbelievably Cute and Fluffy Bunnies?!"

"I'm sure it won't work," Sarah whispered to the others, "but I'm going to try making a wish anyway. It's our only hope."

"Me too," said Charlie.

"It's all I ever wanted to do," agreed Captain Doom.

"Hmmmm hmmmm," agreed Ethel, still

sobbing about poor old Harold.

"Count me in!" said Honk.

"Not me," Vlad opposite-agreed. "Stupid idea."

So, Captain Doom, Sarah, Charlie, Ethel, Honk and Vlad all closed their eyes, and, unbeknownst to each other, all silently wished for the exact same thing.

"I wish to have my family back."

But not a single one of them was magically transported to wherever their family might be. No long-lost family members had suddenly appeared either. When they opened their eyes, they saw nothing but anticlimax, disappointment and shark-infested waters.

Nothing had happened. They were all still about to die.

Tenacious Hunt stepped to the side, rested his hand on a large wooden lever, and gave the orders for the head-chopping-offing to begin.

"Raise the blade, please, Lieutenant Snare!"

Lieutenant Snare began pulling on a rope, and

the humongous blade slowly began to rise higher and higher into the air.

"Hang on a minute!" interrupted Sarah, as she looked down the row of heads and noticed that the poo-faced goat-head man was one of them. "Why are you going to chop *his* head off? He's already dead!"

"Nope," said Harold, popping his eyes open and smiling. "Actually I'm not! I'm still alive, Sarah darling. I never did finish telling you what my plan was. You see, what I was going to say, before that rather large goat very rudely landed on my head and momentarily killed me, was that we should all *pretend* to be dead, like animals do. After all, nobody tries to kill someone who's already dead! Except..." He glanced up, sadly, at the head-chopper-offer. "It may be too late for that now. No point in pretending any more, Sarah darling."

Ethel began making loud, happy sobbing noises at the sight of her not-dead husband.

"Hang on..." began Sarah, looking completely baffled. "Why did you just call me *Sarah darling*?"

"Because it's *me*, darling – Grandpa!" chuckled Harold.

"HMMMMMMM!" Ethel cheered in delight.

"Wha...?" said Sarah, struggling to see any resemblance to her grandpa underneath all that poo and crazy hair.

"It really is me. And that's your grandma right beside you!" Harold added, enjoying Sarah's surprise.

"Grandma? Grandpa!" gasped Sarah, still semi-speechless. "It's you? It's you! My wish did come true!" she exclaimed with tears streaming down her face.

"Mine too!" blubbed Charlie.

"HMMMM-HMMM!" agreed Ethel.

"Raise the blade quicker, please, Lieutenant Snare," Tenacious Hunt groaned impatiently. "These lot are beginning to make me fill *sick*."

"And I've been trying to explain this all day,"

continued Harold, "but haven't been able to, what with our mouths being tied shut and everything, but after all these years of seeking revenge for the death of our beloved daughter, we thought that we had found the killer in this man here – Vladimir Death Pirate. But we were wrong. We were so wrong. More wrong than we could ever be. Because Vladimir Death Pirate did not kill our daughter. *Nobody* killed our daughter. Because our dear daughter, your mother, Sarah and Charlie, is still very much alive."

Sarah and Charlie couldn't believe what they were hearing. They *literally* could not believe it. They had known all their lives that their mum was dead; there was no way she could magically be alive now!

"What are you talking about?" Sarah managed to ask in a tiny whisper of a voice.

"Your mother is here with us right now," Harold said, sniffling away as a single tear rolled down his cheek. "Only she doesn't call herself Princess

Grunt any more. She now goes by the name of . . . Captain Doom."

"WwwwwwWHAT?!" said Sarah, her flow of tears suddenly stopping dead. "What are you talking about, Grandpa? My mum's *dead*. And when she was alive, I'm pretty sure she wasn't a *man*!"

"We *thought* she was dead," Harold said, beaming at Captain Doom, who looked just as shell-shocked as Sarah. "We thought we'd lost our dear daughter for ever, but we were wrong, because here she is. And she *is* a woman – a very scary-looking, bearded pirate woman, but a woman all the same."

"Prettiest princess I've ever seen," added Vlad, quite wrongly.

Sarah turned to Charlie.

Charlie turned to Sarah.

"Has everyone gone completely *mad*?!" Charlie whispered.

Sarah and Charlie both turned to Captain Doom, to see what he had to say about all of this nonsense, but to their amazement, he was sobbing and smiling even more than Harold was. And then Captain Doom turned *away* from the twins.

"What is *going on*?" demanded Sarah.

"My neck, Sarah," Captain Doom sobbed. "Take a look at my neck."

There it was, peeking out from beneath Captain Doom's big collar – a little pink seal-shaped birthmark – the Royal Seal.

Sarah and Charlie both gasped in amazement, then Captain Doom turned back to face them.

"Sarah? Charlie?" Captain Doom spluttered. "I can't believe it's you! My dear children! Your grandpa's right – I *am* your mother!"

Sarah and Charlie both squinted hard at Captain Doom. Could it really be that under that beard and fearsome expression was their *mother*?

And then Captain Doo— I mean, *Princess Grunt's* eyes fell upon Honk, who was also sobbing at the heartbreaking reunion. "Is that...? Could it really be...?"

Her voice trailed off into uncontrollable sobs.

My wish came true, too! she thought. *I finally have my family back!*

"Yes." Harold nodded, also gazing at Honk. "It is. We couldn't believe it when we saw him, too. I mean, what were the chances? It didn't seem possible!"

"My beloved husband?" Princess Grunt laughed and cried at the same time. "Prince Mellybottom?"

Everybody cheered, and sobbed, and laughed at the magnificence of such an amazing reunion. Even Tenacious Hunt was having a good chuckle (but only at the name "Prince Mellybottom"). And then, five minutes and eleven seconds later, he was as angry as ever.

"That blade must be in place by now!" he barked at Lieutenant Snare, who instantly stopped laughing and jumped back to work.

"It really is him," beamed Harold, ignoring Tenacious Hunt's outbursts. "Your husband, Grunty darling. And your father, Sarah and Charlie."

Now the whole family were sobbing and smiling and giggling with glee, until Honk suddenly said:

"Actually, sorry, no, you're wrong. My name's Captain Honk, **AAAARGHHH!** SORRY. And before today, I'd never met any of you in my entire life. Sorry to disappoint you."

The smiles suddenly fell from everyone's faces.

"Oh, my mistake," said Harold, sadly. "Sorry, I could have sworn tha—"

"No! It *is* him! He doesn't remember!" Sarah quickly explained. "Something bonked him on the head a long time ago, and he forgot who he was!"

"Of course!" whispered Captain Princess Grunty Doom. "That night on the cliff, the night you two were born... We were sitting on the hilltop. The sun had just gone down, and ... oh, it was so perfect, so romantic, but it was *so dark*... And neither of us could see each other, and your father thought he was kissing me, but he mistook me for a goat's bottom, and it kicked the two of us over the cliff edge. When I woke up, your father was nowhere to be seen, but there was a pirate ship, sailing away from the shore, so I assumed the prophecy had come true, and that he'd been kidnapped by pirates. But he must have hit his head and just wandered off, and..."

Hearing the moment told back to him must have sparked a memory in Honk's mind because, very suddenly, his eyes lit up and he looked happier than anyone had ever seen him.

"I remember!" Honk exclaimed. "The goat's bottom! I remember it! I . . . I kissed it, and then it . . . it farted, I mean it *trumped*, I mean it *HONKED*! It honked in my face! And . . . and it *stank*. Oh, it stank so badly, and then . . . and then, when it kicked me down the cliff, that's when I got this dent in my head. That's when I stopped remembering, until . . . until *now*."

Honk turned to the twins and looked upon them as if he were seeing them for the very first time. And not just that, he did something else for the first time – he actually got their names right!

"Sarah? Charlie? And my darling Princess Grunty-woo?!"

"I searched for you, I really did!" Captain Princess Grunt sobbed to her husband. "I searched for so long, but you were nowhere to be found – and I saw the ship disappearing, so … so I went back to the palace, but…" She turned to the rest of her family. "But you were all gone!"

"We heard the news that you were missing," Harold explained, crying harder than ever. "We thought the witch's prophecy had come true, and that you had been taken from us, and that the babies were in danger too, so we … we left the palace, and hid. I'm so sorry."

"No, don't be sorry, I thought the prophecy had come true too," explained Princess Grunt. "I thought pirates had taken you all! So I went to the docks, and I took a boat, and I made a promise to myself that I would never stop sailing, that I would never stop searching for that fluffy bunny island, that I would destroy any pirate ship that I found, until I had you all back in my arms."

"But how did you become a *pirate*?" asked Charlie, struggling to keep up with all this new information.

"I never *was* a pirate, Charlie. That's just what everyone else called me. I was just a mum, a wife, a daughter, doing her best to get her family back."

"Hang on a minute," said Sarah, her face crumpled with confusion, slowly catching up with what she was hearing. "What do you mean you went to the *palace*? Did you actually *live* in a palace?"

"Ah," said Harold, lowering his head with guilt. "There's something that your grandma and I failed to tell you. The palace was our home, Sarah; you see, your grandma and I ... well, we ... how do I say this? We are, ever so slightly ... the king and queen of Angerland ... which makes you two..."

"I'm a *princess*?!" gasped Sarah. "I'm a real-life PRINCESS?!!"

"And I'm a *prince*?" Charlie whispered, in shock.

"Wait," said Sarah. "Princesses still get to fight with swords, climb trees, and go on adventures, right? Because if I have to be one of those prissy little princesses that..."

"Blah, blah, blah, blah BLAH!" groaned Tenacious Hunt, who had been growing increasingly restless, waiting for his crew to finish preparing the head-chopper-offer. "This is all so very impressive – you all make up a ridiculous story about being the long-lost royals of Angerland, and I'm supposed to believe this rubbish, and say, *Oh, you're the long-lost royals of Angerland? Well, in that case, I must set you all free!* and then you sail off into the sunset and live happily ever after. Well, guess what? YOU'RE STILL ALL GOING TO DIE! And even if you *were* the real royal family of Angerland you'd still all die, because you're still all pirates! And it is my duty, bestowed upon me by the *real* queen of Angerland, some twenty years ago, to destroy *ALL PIRATES*! Royal ones or not! So quit your yapping, and let's get on with this head-chopping-offing!"

"Excuse me!" barked Honk, I mean Mellybottom.

"We are trying to have a family reunion here, and if you don't mind…"

"Right, that's it," snapped Tenacious Hunt. "I'm bored and I'm hungry. Now please be quiet. I'm going to count down from three, then I'm going to pull this lever, and then you can carry on your ridiculous fake reunion at the bottom of the ocean. OK?"

"No, it's not OK!" Harold protested. "We *are* the royal family!"

"Of course you are," Hunt yelled sarcastically. "And I suppose that parrot's actually a fire-breathing dragon?"

"No," retorted Harold, "actually he's…"

My breath caught in my chest. Did Harold know? Did he actually know the truth about my transformation into a parrot? That I was really Sebillius Quark trapped in this birdbrained body? Maybe this was going to be the reunion to beat all reunions!

"He's…" Harold continued, "he's just a silly little parrot. But *we* are the royal family!"

My little bird-sized heart sank down to my little bird-sized feet.

"Three..." Hunt began to count down, not listening to one more word from any of them.

There was nothing for it — all the wishes had been used up and there was no other chance of escape. I knew I had to try another spell...

"Two..." continued Hunt, already beginning to pull on the lever.

I closed my eyes, raised a wing, did a quick turn, and focused like I had never focused before...

"You can't fail them now," I whispered in my head. And then — "UNDO!"

"One."

Tenacious Hunt pulled the lever, and the blade fell down.

CHOP THUD PLOP PLOP PLOP PLOP PLOP PLOP PLOP.

First there was a *SWISH* as the family-sized blade of the head-chopper-offer dropped down.

Then there was a CHOP!

Then there were seven PLOPS as seven heavy lumps splashed into the seven seas.

Then eight plops...

Then nine...

Then ten ... twenty ... fifty ... *hundreds*!

Sarah and Charlie opened their eyes and found, much to their delight, that it wasn't their heads falling into the ocean, but *parts of the boat*!

All the officers of the Secret Sea Police stared, dumbstruck, as the SSP *Destroyer* began to fall to pieces around them and crumble into the sea.

I did it! I told myself in amazement, as gold sparkles rained down around them all. *I did it! I did something to help! I did ... I did ... I actually did MY JOB again!*

OK, so it hadn't gone exactly as planned – the spell that had turned me into a parrot *hadn't* been undone – but all the pegs and bolts and screws that held the SSP *Destroyer* together *had* been undone!

Officers of the SSP ran screaming as masts and sails toppled down around them. Some of them were sent tumbling into the ocean as entire chunks of the boat fell to pieces. There was wood and canvas and limbs everywhere as everyone on board ran for their lives. Everyone, that is, except for Tenacious Hunt. There was only one thing worrying him, and that was his world record for capturing pirate captains.

Amid all the running and screaming and mayhem and panic, Tenacious Hunt emerged with a large chunk of wood in his hands and cut a path directly towards Ethel, who had fallen to the deck and, with her hands still tied behind her back, was struggling to get to her feet.

"I only have to kill three of you!" he boomed.

He raised the jagged lump of wood high up in the air, then swung it down towards Ethel's head.

"I like you," said Vlad as he appeared alongside Hunt and plucked the chunk of wood from his hands while it was still up in the air.

Hunt turned in surprise to see the towering pirate standing right beside him.

Vlad gave a little smile and said, "I hope you live happily ever after," then pushed Tenacious Hunt straight into the shark-infested waters.

Then, as calm as can be, Vlad scooped up a broken length of mast under one arm, scooped up

Ethel under the other, and herded the rest of the royal family to the front of the boat – the only part not yet in the water.

"Nobody hold tight!" Vlad caringly instructed them. "Let's all drown!"

And with that, they all leapt from the boat, straight into the perilous waters, and clung to the mast for dear life.

"What about the sharks!" cried Sarah, spitting water from her mouth.

"I think they've got enough to keep them busy for now," Harold assured her, gesturing towards the dozens of splashing Secret Sea Police behind them.

So Sarah, Charlie, Harold, Ethel, Princess Grunt and Prince Mellybottom all joined Vlad on the big, floating chunk of mast, as they peacefully drifted into the sunset, on their calm and pleasant journey back to Angerland.

NEARLY EIGHT
HOURS LATER

Four hours later Brenda the Executioner, First Mate
Scary Face, Mr Lookout, Frizzy-Haired Karen, and
the rest of crew of the *Bright Pink Ship of Doom*, who
had all been thrown to the beach when they had
crashed into the Island of Unbelievably Cute and
Fluffy Bunnies, were happily rowing along in the
many lifeboats that had survived the crash. Also in
those lifeboats was every scrap of treasure Captain
Doom had ever scavenged, and now it belonged to
her crew, who, being kind and polite as they were,

happily shared it with their fellow survivors – their ex-prisoners, First Mate Ned, Freakishly Tall Pirate Who Hops Too Much, Gigantic Steve and the entire crew of the *Vladiator*, as they all made their way across the seven seas, towards a life of luxury on the Paradise Isles.

Two hours after that, Tenacious Hunt and the Secret Sea Police, who had managed to *not* get eaten in the shark-infested waters (well, most of them, at least), swam to shore on a nearby island, appropriately named Turn Back Now, Run ... Run While You Still Can, where they remained stuck, with no boats, and no way of ever escaping the many horrendous creatures that lived there.

And two hours after *that*, when the sun was beginning to rise again, Vlad and the royal family arrived safely on the shores of Angerland. They were cold, wet and tired, and it was a long walk home, but this didn't seem to bother any of them. In fact all seven of them were the happiest they had been in a long, long time. They had so much to talk about, so much to catch up on, yet none of them did much speaking as they trudged homeward.

Honk was too lost in the never-ending stream of memories, which were flooding back by the second, to do any talking.

I remember my first day at school! he cheered to himself. *I remember the time I laughed soup out of my nose! I remember I have absolutely no interest in being a pirate whatsoever! And I can remember my real name!*

And, on remembering his real name, he laughed for five minutes and eleven seconds.

Princess Grunt was in too much shock to even string a sentence together. She had been working non-stop, I mean *literally* non-stop, for ten years, trying to get her family back. And with each passing day of those ten years, she felt less and less confident about ever finding them. So now that she had found them, *all* of them, in one single day, she found that she was genuinely lost for words. And she remained lost for words for many hours to come.

Sarah, who for the first time ever was walking

hand in hand with her mum and dad, was enjoying the moment far too much to talk. There were only twelve words her brain could muster; twelve words that kept going round and round in her head – *this is what it feels like to have a mum and dad*.

Something kept going round and round in Charlie's head, too, but it wasn't *words*, it was a *moment* – a moment that had filled him with pride and self-worth, a moment that confirmed to him that, if he put his mind to it, he really could do anything, and above all, it was a moment that made him realize that he really wasn't a useless little baby, he was more of a hero than Tenacious Hunt *ever* was. *I was BRAVE,* Charlie told himself in delight. *I stood up to the zombunnies! I protected my family! And I did it all without anybody's help!*

It was a moment, among many others, that Harold and Ethel had not failed to notice (well, Harold had because he'd been a little bit dead at the time, but Ethel told him all about it, after Vlad had finally undone her ropes on the way back to Angerland). Harold and Ethel's hearts swelled a little as they trekked, arm in arm, along the narrow, rocky path back home, gazing upon their happily reunited family. All their hard work had finally paid off – training Sarah and Charlie to fend for themselves, keeping their identities hidden from dangerous pirates, and managing to bring Princess Grunt and Prince Mellybottom back from the dead. The worst had finally happened, and everyone had lived to tell the tale. Having spent so long feeling that they had failed in their duties as parents, as grandparents, and as *king and queen*, Harold and Ethel finally felt that they had managed to do something right.

The whole family was overjoyed. They were back together! Their wishes really had come true.

But there were two people whose wishes had *not* come true – *I* had not returned to my human form, and *Vlad* had not found his dad. But it wasn't actually as disappointing as it sounds. Especially after what Ethel said next:

"You're welcome to stay with us, if you wish, Mr

Death Pirate," she kindly told Vlad as she linked her arm into his. "To *live* with us, I mean. In fact we'd all be rather sad if you *didn't*. After all we've been through together, you're like a member of the family now, you *and* your parrot friend."

And this was all Vlad really needed to hear. You see, what he had actually been searching for was that warm and cosy feeling of being loved and understood by a family, and, well, that was exactly what he *had* found. It may not have been *his* family, but they seemed to love and understand him all the same (much more than his dad ever had, at least!). In fact, the more Vlad thought about it, the more he began to remember that his dad was never really loving or understanding in the first place! He was more ... *mean* and *manipulative*, and a little bit too obsessed with smashing kittens and **WORLD DOMINATION.**

I perched on Vlad's shoulder as he pulled that map from his pocket, gazed at that ever-elusive X, and wondered where in the world it might be. If only I could have spoken, I would have told him the truth – that the X never had actually led to his dad, it had only ever led to the place where his dad had stolen him from – his *real* home, a country named Angerland.

But Vlad didn't seem to need me to tell him this. He must have felt it in his bones because, there and then, he tore that map into little pieces and, with a smile, threw them into the wind.

"No thank you," he told Ethel, with a smile. "I don't think my parrot and I would like living here, would we?" As he turned to me for an answer, it took me a moment to remember that he meant the opposite of what he had said. "I don't even like this parrot! He's stupid, he has no idea what's going on, he almost killed us all, and we have nothing in common."

My heart began to melt. It was the nicest thing anyone had ever said about me, and I voiced my approval with a soft "Squark!"

Maybe being a parrot isn't such a bad thing after all, I thought. *Besides, how many wizards get to do the things I've done and see the things I've seen?*

How many wizards get to FLY?

I gave Vlad's shoulder a brotherly squeeze with my claws, and Vlad gave me a loving pat on the head, and I knew that this was going to be the beginning of a fantastic friendship, a thought that Vlad clearly shared when he said:

"Little parrot, I think I'm going to hate you for the rest of my life."

(He meant the opposite, of course.)

So there we were – a parrot and a pirate – the perfect pairing.

Now that everyone felt part of a family, life was going to be perfect, and they all knew it. Well, everyone except Sarah, who was wondering: *How are seven people possibly going to fit in our tiny little cottage?*

But as they turned the next corner of the narrow little path, the answer to that question revealed itself – they weren't going back to the tiny little cottage at all. They were the royal family of Angerland. They were going to live in Angerland

Palace, of course! The very same palace that was now directly in front of them.

Sarah and Charlie gawped at the magnificent structure and the city that lay around it, and they suddenly realized why Harold and Ethel had spent so many Sundays teaching them the history of Angerland – it was to prepare them for their jobs as prince and princess of the realm, and, one day, *rulers* of the realm. They couldn't begin to imagine what their new lives would have in store for them. They couldn't even begin to imagine what their new *home* would have in store for them! It was at least five hundred times bigger than their cottage! It was a palace that defied imagination – it was so tall that it touched the clouds, so vast that it filled their entire field of vision, so intricate, with towers, walkways, bridges, and turrets, and more turrets, and turrets upon turrets upon turrets, and the whole thing seemed to be lit up by a magical glow.

"Welcome home," Ethel whispered into the night.

And they all marched forth, towards their new lives together, with love in their hearts and a spring in their steps, and they all lived *very* happily ever aft—

Erghhh!

Yuck!

No!

I forgot how soppy the end of this story was!

Let's just skip to the bit where it says "The end"...

THE END

(kind of ...)

THE LAST CHAPTER IN THIS STORY-TYPE THING

So that's it. One of the top six stories never to have been told. And now it *has* been told. Not very well, though, sorry. But hey, what do you expect when your narrator is a parrot?

I know what you're thinking: *I wish I could move things using just the power of my mind.* Or maybe: *What would the world be like if lemons were called yellows?* We all think these things from time to time (well, maybe not the lemons thing). But what you *should* be thinking is: *Is that it?! THAT'S the end???! I want to know what happened next! What happened with Vlad's dad? Did Prince Mellybottom's memory come back completely? Did Sebillius ever turn back into a human being? Did Harold and Ethel ever get a haircut? I want some answers! That was a terrible ending!*

Well, for once, that isn't my fault. That's just where the story ends. Don't blame *me*. I didn't write it! I'm just *telling it*, and that's how it happened. There's not really anything else I can say.

That's it.

The end.

It was nice meeting you.

Goodbye.

Please close the book and walk away.

Stop reading.

Why are you still reading?

It's over!

There's nothing left of the story!

I have no more to tell you!

Why would you continue to...

Ooh! I just remembered something. . .!

You know that award that Tenacious Hunt was so desperate to win? Well, it turns out his brother didn't win it either. Someone stole it, just minutes before the ceremony, and replaced it with a pirate flag that had a note attached to it:

From the one pirate you will never capture.
Death

Weird, right?

Oh well, that really is it now. I genuinely have nothing more to tell you.

This is definitely the end.

For real.

I mean it.

I am not going to write *any* more words on this page.

Apart from these ones.

And these.

And. . .

THE END

Seriously.

I'm not joking this time.

There is absolutely no more story to tell!

Well, there *is*, but it's not part of *this* story.

I'm finished.

And so is this book.

Look, it must be the end because the words are in the middle of the page.

THE END!

How many times do I have to tell you?

THE END! THE END! THE END!!!

THE END!

THEEEEEEEE
ENNNNNNNNNDUH!

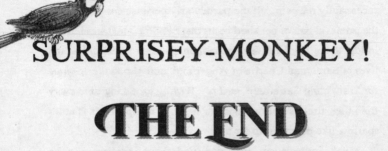

SURPRISEY-MONKEY!

THE END

ACKNOWLEDGEMENTS

I would like to thank Sebillius Quark for taking the time, all those hundreds of years ago, to document this highly important slice of history. I would also like to thank his descendants – Robin and Phoenix – for granting me permission to adapt it for this publication. Thanks must also be given to the *Museum of Ancient Texts* for successfully removing all the particularly pertinacious particles of the primeval pair of perished pants that Sebillius's text was hidden inside, to the *Daniel Foley Foundation*, for their research into the lives of Sarah and Charlie of Angerland, and also to the *Institute for Translating Extremely Scribbly Writing* for taking time away from their tireless work on doctors' notes, to decipher Mr Quark's sparrow-like penmanship for me.

Much appreciation, adulation, and thanksification must be given to the many authors who, with their storytelling talents that far outstrip Mr Quark's or my own, have kept this portion of history alive by writing their own fictional takes on this era. I'm sure that any extremely uncanny similarities between their books and this one are purely coincidental, and have absolutely nothing to do with anyone falling in love with anyone else's work and accidentally on purpose "borrowing" any lovely, shiny ideas from them (also known as "Magpie-ing").

And finally, my endless gratitude must also go to Professor Archibald McFeathergills for telling me to "make sure you use the word 'incredulous' if you want your book to sound clever and stuff".

P.S. – Apologies about the incredulous poo stain